Christmas by the Sea

KC McCormick Çiftçi

One

Eleven Months Before

Hazel sipped her matcha latte, trying not to look directly across the table where her brother was leaning over to whisper into his new girlfriend's ear. Jack and Claire—Claire *Davis*, she reminded herself, still stunned that one of her favorite authors was sitting in her favorite cafe with her—had settled into a comfortable, if not sickeningly sweet, relationship after a whirlwind international romance the previous Christmas. It was simultaneously easy to be around them because they were two of her favorite people and the sort of uncomfortable that she was never able to hide on her too expressive face.

"Jack, stop. She's grimacing again." Claire pushed Jack back into his chair, clicking her tongue at him. "Hazel is never going to want to do anything with us if you can't learn to keep your hands to yourself."

"Considering that I grew up with him...well, good luck teaching him that lesson." Hazel winced at her own words. "I...that sounded creepy. I just meant that he was the actual king of crossing the imaginary line in the car and holding a finger, like, a quarter of an inch from my eyeball, the whole time insisting he wasn't touching me."

"This is true," Jack admitted. "I've been told to keep my hands to myself approximately since the day Hazel was born." He picked Claire's hand up from the table and kissed the back of her knuckles. "But if anyone can finally teach me, it'll be you." He looked over Claire's hand to his little sister. "She's that good."

"I *know* she's good." Hazel grumbled the words with more aggression than she felt. "I've been reading her words longer than you've been hearing them."

"Now, now, my dear Holloways." Claire took her hand back from Jack, then gave them each a stern look in turn. "Can we all just get along? Can the two of you resist the urge to snipe at each other at least long enough for us to drink our coffees?"

"I know *I* can," Hazel mumbled into her to-go cup. "Good luck with him, though."

Something unspoken passed between Jack and Claire, an urging eyebrow lift, a hiss that was almost a whisper. Finally, Claire sighed and turned her attention to Hazel. "How are you doing, Haze? With the whole Daniel situation, I mean. Have you talked to him?"

The bottom dropped out of Hazel's stomach at the reminder of her old friend, her first crush, the unrequited love of her life. The first time she had spoken to Claire on the phone had been in the midst of the crisis of confessing her feelings to him, only to confirm that they were not even remotely reciprocated. Claire had been the voice of reason talking her out of continuing to try to convince Daniel that they were meant to be. And yet...

"Yeah, we've been talking. Things are good. Fine. Really good, actually." She lifted her cup again, hiding her mouth behind it, creating a barrier between herself and Claire so that the other woman might not read into the truth underneath her words.

But if Claire was intuitive, then Jack was experienced, and a lifetime of reading his little sister's hidden truths and white lies wouldn't steer him wrong. "I call bullshit," he said, sipping his own coffee.

Claire wheeled to face him. "What do you mean?" She looked back to Hazel, her eyebrows climbing her forehead. "What does he mean? What are you two talking about?"

Jack responded before Hazel could. "She means, if I'm reading things accurately, that things are back to normal with her and Daniel. Back to the way they were before, I'm guessing?" When Hazel nodded at his question, he sighed. "So, they're spending just as much time together as they ever did, and Hazel's heart is right back where it was before."

"Is it really, Hazel?" Claire's tone was gentle, her soft eyes waiting for Hazel to look into them. "I don't mean any judgment. Just...is Jack right? You still have feelings for Daniel?"

Hazel blew out a long exhale, finally replacing her cup on the table and looking up into the expectant eyes of her brother and Claire. There was concern on Claire's face, a matching set with what was on Jack's, though her brother had added a heavy sprinkle of frustration. This wasn't his first rodeo, after all.

"It was good to spend some time away from him," she said. Hazel hadn't seen Daniel for two weeks after her big love confession, and he had given her the space she needed during that time. "I think it was healing for me. I realized I needed to spend more energy on myself, on my own growth. Not worry so much about him. So...when he texted me and asked if we could hang out, if we could be friends again, it sounded like a good idea. I was in a better place, and there's no reason at all why the two of us can't be friends."

"No..." Claire left the word hanging, ready to retrieve it if Hazel's speech took a turn down the wrong path.

"So you two have been having fun, and the old feelings are creeping back in...right?" Jack followed her words to their logical conclusion. "The same thing that happened when you went off to college?"

Hazel winced. "That was different. We were teenagers, and everyone knows the summer before college is the perfect time to tell someone about the secret crush you've had on them. It's not like there was any pressure there, any expectation that he would drop out of his school and follow me to NYU or anything."

"No, but it did make things super awkward between the two of you." Jack took another sip of his coffee. "And it sent you down a real spiral, like you were grieving what could have been between the two of you. Of course, by the time you met up for Christmas—starting that damn annual Christmas tradition of yours—you were all too ready to fall right back into that old familiar trap. That's as much a part of your tradition as any of the rest of it."

"Hey. That's not fair." Hazel's lip wobbled as Jack's words hit their mark. It wasn't like him to be this brutal in his honesty. "Every year we meet up for a Christmas drink, but I don't, like, drink too much and reveal my undying love for him." As she finished her sentence, a memory came into focus. "Well, not *every* year, at least."

"It's okay, Haze." Jack sighed as he reached over to pat the back of her hand. "He's a great guy, and we all love him. And it's not like everyone doesn't joke about the two of you ending up together. I can see how it would be confusing."

Claire spoke up then. "Everyone jokes about that? Even after all this time?" When the siblings nodded, she moved around the table to sit next to Hazel, encircling her shoulder with an arm. "I'm so sorry. Oblivious families are the worst."

"Nobody is trying to be cruel," Hazel responded, "but yeah...I mean, I guess it is a little bit annoying that they keep teasing." Still, who was she to second guess the wisdom of two entire families? If everyone, from her own father to Daniel's grandmother, was convinced the two of them were destined to get married one day, then maybe they were on to something. Daniel might be more open to the idea if he heard it so many times, especially if he heard it from the same people he trusted to give him advice about other things, like his career...

"What are you thinking right now?" Her brother's question interrupted her thoughts, his gaze trained on her forehead as if he could read the thoughts inside her head. "I know daydreaming when I see it, and I've got a bad feeling about this."

Hazel sighed. "It's fine, Jack. Really. Everyone knows—or at least thinks—that the two of us are destined to end up together some distant day down the road, so what's the harm in me thinking that too? If anything, you should be having this conversation with Daniel, since he's apparently the only human left in existence who is unconvinced of that fact."

Claire lifted her head from where it had been resting on Hazel's shoulder, giving her an apologetic smile. "And me," she said. "I'm not convinced either."

"Ouch." If there was ever a person you should be assured of getting on board with your dreams of romance and impossible love stories, it should be the romance author in your life. If even she couldn't see it...

"I just think..." Claire paused as she took a steadying breath, a glance exchanged with Jack. "I just think that if it were going to happen between the two of you, then it would have already. If there was something there, on his part, I mean...wouldn't it already *be* there? Sure, he might need some time to confess his undying love, to admit it even to himself, but how long does that really take? He's had plenty of opportunities."

"I don't think there's actually a time limit on it." Hazel crossed her arms over her chest, sniffing. "You both must know that people are all different, that love stories are all unique. And I know the connection I have with Daniel is special. I know it the way I know...well, the way I know anything I'm really sure about. I'm okay with us not being together now because I'm so sure that's how it's all going to turn out in the future. We understand each other, and I know he loves me as a friend. I know how lucky we are to have each other. It's just a matter of time."

Jack and Claire were looking at each other, an intensity in the message they were communicating nonverbally that pushed Hazel from the realms of politeness into outright frustration. She got to her feet, picking up her matcha and tilting her head towards the door. "I should go. Got some errands to run while I'm downtown. Let's do this again soon."

Before she could slip away, Claire was hugging her, and then Jack took his turn. "We didn't say any of this to hurt you, Haze," her brother mumbled against her ear. "We care about you. Don't want you to get hurt. Actually want you to get all the great things you deserve in life."

She forced a smile as she stepped back. "Don't worry about me, guys. The fact is, I know what I deserve, and I'm confident I'm going to get it. It's okay if no one else can see it or can even believe that I see it. It's all really going to be okay."

She made a beeline for the door, refusing to linger a moment longer to take in the worried looks shared between her brother and his girlfriend. They meant well, that much was clear, but it was still insulting to get their pity and frustrating that no one else could see what she did. Everything was fine, as far as she and Daniel were concerned. And they would all see one day. They would all, finally, know that she had been right and that two best friends really *could* fall in love with each other, even if it took decades for it to happen.

Hazel ducked into another shop, killing time. She hadn't actually had any errands to run, but sitting at the cafe with

Jack and Claire had quickly become unbearable. Instead, she wandered the aisles of her favorite bookstore—exercising impressive self control by not buying anything, though her camera roll was now full of new covers to add to her TBR—and done some window shopping at a boutique that was well out of her price range. Still, she wasn't quite ready to head home yet.

She pulled out her phone, took a deep breath, and then called Daniel.

He answered on the second ring. "Hey, Craze," he said, a smile in his voice as he used the nickname he'd given her in middle school, one that had made an unfortunate comeback in recent days. "How's it going? What's up?"

"It's good, yeah. I'm in the city, actually. Any chance you're free to meet up?" Daniel's apartment wasn't far from where she was walking, not more than a few subway stops, but she would go there on foot if it meant getting to spend some time together.

Daniel sucked his teeth. "I'm sorry, Craze. I'm super busy today. Just about to head out to pick up a few things. We've got a work event tonight, so you know that means I need to dress to impress." Daniel worked in the sales department for the Schuler Group, a real estate development group.

"Of course." *I'm not going to ask him to invite me along, not to the shopping or to the work event. I have my own plans, my own life...right? I don't need to be anyone's plus one.*

"What are you doing tonight?" Daniel asked, as if he could hear her thoughts. Was he about to invite her to join him?

"No plans, actually. Looks like my future holds sweatpants and a good book, maybe a glass of wine."

"I'm jealous. That sounds great, actually."

"I guess it all depends on how you look at it. From where I'm sitting, it seems kind of boring, but I guess that's just because I haven't been getting out enough lately." How much harder could she hint that she was desperate for plans, for a reason to throw on a nice dress and do some mingling?

"Now now, Hazel. You should be grateful you don't have to go to actually boring things, like this event of mine. I mean, I'm sure the food will be decent, but it's not as if schmoozing potential clients is the most intellectually stimulating way to spend an evening."

"No, you're right." The drop in her stomach was a physical reminder that Daniel wasn't going to save her, that he was her best friend who loved to tease her and *not* her boyfriend who was attuned to her emotions and ready to rescue her from any situation she didn't love. Still, maybe he could help her out with one thing...

"Daniel?" She cut into his diatribe about schmoozing, her tone bringing his complaining to an abrupt halt.

"What's up, Craze? Something on your mind?"

Apart from the fact that you've got to stop calling me that? Sure. "Uh, it's just...we're going to be okay, right?"

"What do you mean?" She heard the concern in his voice, and she smiled at the reminder that he did, in fact, care.

"Just with...you know, my inconvenient feelings. Liking you. The stuff we talked about before." For once, she was grateful to be talking to him on the phone rather than face-to-face, where her bright red cheeks would have been impossible to hide.

"Of course we are. It's not a problem for me if it's not a problem for you. Plus, that's old news, right?"

"Er...right." She winced, wishing the feelings were as distant a memory as he seemed to think they were. "My brother just sort of got into my head, I guess. So I wanted to check with you. Confirm for myself that we were going to be fine."

Daniel laughed. "With no disrespect to Jack, he's never really understood our friendship. I wouldn't expect him to start now. But it's okay, Hazel. Really. Everybody gets crushes sometimes, and they go away eventually. I'm not going to make things weird and you don't need to either. Okay?"

Hazel gritted her teeth as she nodded, at war within herself about something Daniel had said, something that wasn't landing quite right. "Okay," she said, finally. "I'm glad we agree."

Two

December

"I can't believe you aren't going to be here for Holloway pizza making," grumbled Claire from where she was sitting at the end of Hazel's bed. "Especially not my first one. What are we going to do without you?"

Hazel looked up from her phone. "You'll make—and then, more importantly, eat—delicious pizza. It's fairly straightforward, Claire. I think you can handle it." She turned her attention to her brother, who had just entered the room. "And don't you dare give me a hard time about missing Christmas, not after what you did last year. I learned it from watching you, big bro."

Jack waited until his hands were empty, handing a cup of hot chocolate in turn to Claire and then Hazel, before shrugging. "I think it worked out just great for me, so I wouldn't even dream of giving you a hard time about it." He took a seat next to Claire, patting her softly on the knee as something unspoken passed between them.

"Right." Hazel set her hot chocolate on the desk and got to her feet, surveying the chaos that was her bedroom, her clothes strewn over every surface and her open—and *empty*—suitcase yawning next to the bed. "Who wants to help me pack?"

"Not it," said Jack. "Drink your hot chocolate while it's hot, Haze. We can keep strategizing and then the packing will be super speedy."

She dropped back into her chair with a sigh, only too happy to oblige. "Right? The more thorough my to-be-packed list is, the quicker the job is bound to be. That's right, isn't it?"

Claire nodded in earnest. "Oh, absolutely. I'm a huge fan of packing from a list. Of course, somehow I still end up packing only clothes I hate in my first attempt and then tearing the whole thing apart and starting over again." She shrugged. "And I still end up forgetting something or packing for entirely the wrong weather. What is the temperature supposed to be like in Antalya, anyway?" She tugged the collar of her turtleneck higher, giving Hazel the briefest pang of guilt for not cranking the thermostat up in her apartment, a pang which faded as soon as she thought of her last gas bill.

"It's supposed to be really nice and mild," she said, pulling up the weather app on her phone. "No rain in the 10-day forecast, but it's also not exactly warm enough that I'm going to pack my swimsuit." She looked up. "No, that's crazy. I should always pack my swimsuit, shouldn't I?"

"If you learned anything from that family vacation to Buffalo where you were the only one not splashing around in the Holiday Inn's indoor pool, then yeah. If you didn't learn that particular lesson, then no, I guess."

"Thanks, Jack. Very helpful, and not at all a painful reminder of a trip I'd like to pretend never happened." Still, Hazel added "swimsuit" to the bottom of the packing list in her phone's notes app.

In just a few days, Hazel would be boarding a plane to Antalya, Turkey, with none other than her oldest and dearest friend, Daniel Martin. She was still pinching herself at the thought of the two of them going on an international adventure together, leaving their families and other friends behind to celebrate Christmas in a vastly different locale than they were accustomed to for the holidays.

Hazel's parents had been far from thrilled when she had first shared her plans with them, but they had insisted it wasn't about her missing out on a family holiday. "I don't care about that," her mom had said with a wave of her hand. "We can celebrate Christmas together anytime. We can do it in March if that's the first time I can get my kids together. At least we wouldn't have to shovel snow then." A pause. "Well, we *might* have to shovel snow in March. Better make it April, just to be safe."

"What's the problem, then?" Hazel had asked.

"I'm just worried about you," her mom had answered, stroking Hazel's hair. "I don't want you to get hurt. And flying off to the beach with a handsome man who we all know you have unreciprocated feelings for sounds like the perfect way to get very hurt." A sigh. "It's not that we don't love Daniel. You know we do. We love the whole Martin family." She leaned closer, her voice for Hazel's ears only. "I just love you more. You're my priority."

Hazel had forced a smile. "It isn't like that, Mom. For one thing, it's not like every trip with a beach involved is going to be some kind of honeymoon fantasy. It's going to be chilly, and my heart will be protected behind layers of scarves and cardigans."

Mrs. Holloway had given her a tight-lipped smile. "Good."

"And also, it's just...well, it's just not going to be romantic. Daniel is going to be doing work things, and I'm going to be on my own, finding ways to entertain myself. It's going to be fine. You just have to trust me."

"Of course I trust you. I'm just afraid that you don't care about protecting your heart the same way I do. And I don't want to watch you march courageously towards something that is going to hurt you."

There hadn't been much Hazel could say after that. It didn't matter that she knew things were going to be different—and she certainly couldn't share her confidence that, one day, it was all going to work out between her and Daniel, with her mother. Not unless she had wanted to see that furrow on her mom's brow grow deep enough to hold a coin. No one understood, not in her family especially, and she had given up on trying to make them. They would all see one day, of that she was sure. In the meantime, all she could do was be patient with them.

And that she could do. If unrequited love had given her one gift, it was the gift of patience. Hazel Holloway was nothing if not highly skilled at waiting to get what she wanted.

Still, as she took in the sight of her brother, so happily enamored by the woman leaning into his shoulder, she felt that not unfamiliar clanging in her chest. What if everyone else was right? What if there was no grand "aha" moment waiting on the horizon where Daniel would finally realize that what he was looking for had been right under his nose the entire time? What if this connection that she thought was so special between them was nothing in comparison to an actual spark, like the one between Jack and Claire?

"Right." She placed her nearly full mug on the desk and got to her feet, striding towards her closet. This was no time to wait and give her doubts and feelings the chance to overwhelm her. This was the time for action, to keep moving towards her goal—towards the moment when she finally boarded the plane and knew this was really happening—and no theoretical packing list could possibly compare with actually stuffing her suitcase full of all her favorite clothes.

Hazel's phone lit up with an incoming call from Daniel a few hours later, well after Jack and Claire had returned to their cocoon of domestic bliss, and a familiar thrill of excitement accompanied the glow of his name above the profile photo she had snapped of him years before.

"Hey." She forced her voice to sound casual, her oldest and most familiar habit of trying to stuff her outsized emotions into a more palatable package. "What's up, Daniel?"

On the other end of the phone, her best friend's sigh was exhausted. "Just a long day, Craze. And when I was driving home at the end of it, I couldn't help but look at all the other commuters and think what lucky jerks they all are since, for most of them at least, this was probably their last day of work until the new year. I can't believe they're making me work over the holidays."

Hazel bit her lip, taking a moment before speaking her truth. Finally, she hedged towards what she thought he needed to hear, infusing her words with a little extra gentility. "I mean, Daniel." She cleared her throat. "They're sending you to an all-inclusive resort in one of the most beautiful cities in the world. It isn't exactly like you've got to pull a double shift in the coal mine."

He laughed, but there was a coldness to it. "I know that. And I'm sure it will be nice there, too. We might even have some fun. It's just totally bananas to me that the company would schedule a corporate retreat over Christmas. Make it make sense, Hazel."

She warmed at the sound of her name on his lips, rare enough given his propensity for using his affectionate, if borderline offensive, nickname instead. "At least they're letting everyone bring their families. That part kind of makes up for it, doesn't it?" Daniel had worked for the Schuler Group since they had graduated from college, and in a truly baffling move, the company had scheduled an end of the year retreat in Antalya. Given that it was the company's 50-year anniversary, and that they had been tending toward record profits that year, Hazel found the decision far less shocking than Daniel apparently did. Plus, she couldn't ignore the fact that all the employees who were invited on the retreat had been free to bring their partners and children as well. Those, like Daniel, who were single and child-free, had still gotten a plus one, and that was how Hazel had found herself staring down the barrel of an international Christmas on the beach.

"Well, bud," she finally said, "I think it's safe to assume that this trip is going to be a lot more fun if you get on board with it than if you keep complaining about how unfair it all is. Because, really...it might be super fun, actually. I don't think they arranged this whole thing to torture their employees. I think it's supposed to be a good time, a reward for all your hard work, a celebration of all the company has accomplished."

"Are you sure you don't work for our public relations department?" Daniel's voice was tinny as it cut into her speech. "You're really good at spinning things to make the Schuler Group sound like it's always doing the right thing."

"Believe it or not, I'm perfectly happy working as a teacher. Plus, it works out pretty nicely that I already have this time of the year off. So, you know, if this becomes a regular thing for the Schuler Group, then I should always be able to join you."

"Right. Er..." There was a tension in Daniel's tone then, something different from what had been there a moment ago. He coughed once. "I mean, that's great. If...you know...if I'm single, then yeah, definitely. You'd be the one I asked." He chuckled. "But God, I hope I'm not still single the next time they do one of these. If I'm still single *and* still working at the Schuler Group in ten years, then it is definitely time to officially declare myself a failure at life."

Hazel winced at his words. "I hardly think either of those things would qualify you as a loser. But if you're still single in ten years and you're really that upset about it, then we could just get married." She clamped her lips shut as soon as the sentence was out. *What was she thinking? Was it too soon to make a joke like that? Would he even believe it was a joke, at this point in their friendship and after she had confessed her feelings for him more times than any woman with a shred of self respect should do?* "I mean—"

"Craze, it's not going to happen," Daniel cut in. "You know that, right?" He sighed, and his exhaustion cut through the distance between them. "You and me, I mean. We're friends, Hazel, and I need you to know that we're just friends. That we aren't going to make some kind of ridiculous marriage pact or anything like that. You're the most important person in my life, the most stable thing I can count on, and I just need to know that you're always going to be that."

How could you be the most important person in someone's life and also the one they were absolutely convinced they would never be anything more than friends with? How could that "truth" even make sense? "I know, Daniel. I think I was making a joke." Her voice was small now, sapped of all energy she had felt a moment before.

"I know," he said, gentler than before. "I just worry sometimes that you're missing out on your real life because you're waiting on me. And I don't think I can ever be what you want me to be. I can't change the way I feel."

"Well, maybe I can't change the way I feel, either," she said, surprised by her own boldness. "So maybe we should both just let each other be, you know? It isn't really your concern what my feelings are. I'm not asking you to be different. I'm not begging you to love me or anything like that."

"No, but..." He sighed. "It's just...it's so hard to know that you're feeling something that means that my behavior could hurt you. I mean...what happens if I meet someone in Turkey? How is that going to work?"

She recoiled at the thought, a possibility for their impending trip that hadn't yet occurred to her. "That would be fine. It's not like I'd want you to bring someone back to the hotel, but that's just because we're sharing a room. But sure...meet someone. Ask her out for a drink. Take her out to dinner. You're free to do all of that. And so am I."

His next laugh had a hardness to it. "Well, we both know you aren't going to do that. It's just...look. I don't know what I can do to make you stop having these feelings for me, but I don't exactly want to try to push you away or hurt you. You're my best friend, and I care about you."

"I'll do a better job hiding them," she said through gritted teeth. "I'll be more careful not to make dumb jokes about us getting married someday. I can't promise to change the way I feel, but I *can* promise to be better about not showing it to you."

"That's not what I want. Not what I'm asking you to do."

"No, but you're asking for something impossible from me. This is what I can give you." In that moment, it was almost impossible to believe that this was the man she loved. Did she have so little self respect that she could hold on to feelings for someone who so clearly did not want them directed his way? Was there really something so irresistible about him that no bad behavior or unkindness on his part could extinguish her hopes?

"Let's just forget about it, Daniel. We're going to have a great trip, and we really don't need to talk about this anymore. Let's just move on."

Three

*I*t's going to be okay, Hazel reminded herself. *It's not like you've never done this before.* She hefted her bag onto the scale at the check-in counter, smiling with unfeigned relief as the number registered in the red LED lights. As much as she had attempted not to stress pack everything in her wardrobe, the last 48 hours hadn't exactly been the picture of ease and domestic bliss.

Daniel cleared his throat next to her, and when she glanced his way, he gave her a tight-lipped smile, which she returned. "Cutting it pretty close to the limit there, eh, Holloway?" He nodded at the suitcase. "What did you even bring? We're only going to be gone for two weeks."

The ticket agent made an admonishing sound as she shook her head. "A gentleman should never question how much a lady has packed. Especially not his girlfriend, and especially not when it's the most wonderful time of the year."

"It's not—"

"We're not—"

Hazel and Daniel had spoken at the same time, tripping over themselves to keep any misunderstanding of the nature of their relationship from sabotaging its delicate ecosystem. Since the awkward ending of their last conversation, Hazel had been working overtime to play it easy and breezy with Daniel, sending him memes and pretending to be interested when he had shared gossip about their old classmates. What she would have preferred to do, either shaking him by the shoulders and demanding to know why he was so sure he wouldn't—*couldn't*—love her or retreating under her coziest comforter for a wallowing session that bordered on hibernation, weren't options. It was better to keep things lighthearted, to move past her latest declaration at such a speed that very soon neither one of them would be able to see even its faintest glint in the rearview mirror of life.

Thankfully, Daniel had played along—or, and Hazel could barely let herself entertain the possibility, he genuinely found it that easy to move on from her vulnerability and rejection. Either way, they had laughed and smiled and bumped shoulders and teased. It was only when someone who didn't know them mistakenly referred to them as a couple that things got awkward.

On second thought, maybe being his plus one over the holidays, when everyone else is going to have their significant others and families around, wasn't the brightest move. But if it was ever too late to realize something like that, then at the airport immediately after checking your bag was that time. All Hazel could do was grit her teeth into an approximation of a smile and hope that repetition would lead to desensitization, and by the end of the trip, they would be laughing sincerely at any mistaken identities.

"Have a nice trip," said the ticket agent, sliding their passports and boarding passes across the counter. "You're all set."

As they walked towards security, Hazel forced herself to maintain a distance between herself and Daniel, even when all she wanted to do was to be drawn right into his gravitational pull. That had always been the problem between them, as far as her heart was concerned. It was so easy to be close to him, to want to be ever closer, and before he had told her for the first time that he just wanted to be friends, her heart had believed that he wanted her to be ever-approaching the limit of closeness. That he wanted exactly what she wanted.

But that wasn't entirely fair, was it? It wasn't, after all, as if Daniel had been playing with her or teasing her with something manufactured. He really *did* love her, and he really did love being close with her, sharing so much of his life with her. He never flinched away from having her by his side, but would instead throw his arm around her shoulder and pull her even closer.

It was only when he had learned the true nature of her feelings for the first time—and every time after that, when she had reminded them both of those feelings—that he had tried to create some distance between them. Those were the times when he kept her at arm's length. The worst thing about it was that she knew he was doing it because she couldn't be trusted to handle the closeness between them, remembering all along that their relationship was purely platonic. If he had been pushing her away because he was disgusted by her or embarrassed by her love, it would have been easier to move on...*probably*. It wasn't as if she had ever figured out how to move on from him.

She hoped she would figure it out one day.

No, that wasn't true. For all the confidence Hazel felt that the grand reveal was still coming, the moment where Daniel would have the veil lifted from his eyes and finally realize that *this* was actually what love was and that what he had been looking for out there in the world didn't even exist...for all that confidence, there wasn't even a vacant corner of her heart that hoped she would ever get over him. How could she, when he was her one chance at true happiness?

"You packed something for the Christmas party, right?" Daniel's question cut into her thoughts. "I highlighted it on the itinerary, but I never asked."

Hazel nodded as they joined the end of the security line snaking through the stanchions. "I did. To be fair, though, I packed most of what I own." She pulled her coat closer around her shoulders, the December weather outside the airport threatening to come inside with every opening of the large glass doors. "Apparently it's warmer in Antalya than it is here, but I couldn't leave my cardigan collection behind. Try to come between an East Coast gal and her cable knits and see what happens, I dare you."

Daniel laughed, and something loosened inside her chest at the familiar sound, at the way he tossed back his head. "That's better than the alternative, actually. I thought you might have bypassed checking the forecast entirely and packed like we were going to the Caribbean.

Just because we'll be by the sea doesn't mean it's bikini weather."

"Yeah, but..." Hazel frowned. "It also isn't exactly polar bear swim weather either."

"So that's your way of saying you brought a swimsuit and will be very disappointed if you don't get to use it?"

She nodded. "Pretty much."

Daniel paused before bobbing his head back. "Fair enough. Then I hope you get everything you want."

The Schuler Group had taken care of all the travel arrangements, and Hazel happily settled into her role as a passenger, rather than the travel coordinator. Knowing that someone else had selected which seat would be assigned to her, had chosen which layover length would be the optimal one, and had already arranged their transportation from the airport to the resort allowed her to put up her feet—metaphorically, of course, since the Schuler Group hadn't splashed out for business class seats—and enjoy the journey.

Hazel didn't travel much—in her career as a third grade teacher, there wasn't much of an occasion for it—so none of the allure had worn off for her. If Daniel put on his eye mask and tuned out, she would be leaning over him to look out the window. If he turned up his nose at the meal they were served, she ate every bite after snapping a picture of the cute rectangular tray with everything in its place. The selection of movies available on the entertainment set was so good that she wished the flight was longer before selecting a few to save for the return journey.

All in all, a travel day was a dream for Hazel Holloway, and even Daniel's perpetual grumbling couldn't take away the magic that she experienced. She held up the tiny carton of water on her tray, mouthed "Isn't it cute?" since he wouldn't take off his gigantic headphones even to eat, and then thrilled when he slid his own water carton onto her tray.

"It's way too small, anyway," he complained. "It just makes you thirstier, drinking a tiny cup of water like that."

They spent a couple short hours in the Amsterdam airport—or at least they were short as far as Hazel was concerned. Daniel had rubbed the bridge of his nose, mumbling something about wanting to just be there already, while Hazel had hunted down a stroopwaffel and planned a future hypothetical trip when the tulips were in bloom.

Before the travel day could extend to the point of annoyance for Hazel—and far after it had reached that same point for Daniel—they were descending towards the Antalya airport. As soon as they had broken through the cloud cover, Hazel was leaning over to look at the land they were approaching, and she felt a thrill in her chest at the sight of the bright blue sea, the coastline, the jagged lines of mountains. Even from this height, the pictures she had seen of Antalya didn't do it justice. They were in for a real treat—something almost magical, if her intuition was to be believed. Briefly, Hazel wondered if this would be the time that changed everything between her and Daniel, and then refocused her attention not on the man who was sitting next to her but on the window beside him, the same one he hadn't even glanced at.

"Look, Daniel," she said, nodding towards the window. "I know you're too cool to get excited about something as boring as the deep blue sea, but still. You have to admit that's beautiful."

He glanced up from his phone at her, then leaned forward slightly to look at the sea below. "It is," he said, his tone matter-of-fact as he leaned back. "I'm just ready to land, ready to be there. Not so impressed by the views from the sky when I'd much rather just be down there."

She sniffed. "There's nothing wrong with enjoying both. I know I can't dip my toes in the water from up here, but that doesn't stop me from wanting to look at it."

"I know." Daniel shifted in his seat, pulling away from her. "We should have switched seats."

"I seem to recall a certain someone complaining that his legs were too long for the middle seat, that he simply had to sit by the window."

"That's true." He nodded. "It's still uncomfortable over here, but at least it's slightly better. The middle seat is the worst."

Hazel leaned back, finally fed up with his attitude. "You know, that's a wonderfully insightful thing to say to your friend who just spent the entire day enjoying a selection of the airline's finest middle seats. What is up with you today? Are you determined to find something wrong with everything?"

Daniel winced. "Sorry, Craze. I guess, since this is our first time traveling together, that I'm revealing a side of myself you may have preferred never to know about. As it turns out, I am the world's worst traveler."

"Really?" She leaned towards him and dropped her voice. "You mean…like, officially? Was there a ceremony to award you that title? Do you have some sort of plaque or trophy to commemorate it?"

Despite himself, he laughed at that. "It's unofficial, actually. But I promise once I get my land legs back, take a shower, and eat some decent food, I'll be the Daniel Martin you know and love. Deal?" He held out his hand, and she took it, shaking it once.

"Deal." She grinned back at her oldest friend, trying to ignore the stupid thrill in her stupid chest at his use of the word "love." *He didn't mean it that way, stop being stupid*, she chided herself, but she knew better than anyone that she was too far gone not to get excited about something like that, no matter how small or silly it would have seemed to someone else.

The time between the airplane landing and Hazel and Daniel arriving at their room at the resort passed in a flash. Maybe it was the normal way of international travel, with every new stage following on the heels of the one before it. They had barely exited the plane and then they were going through passport control, collecting their bags, passing through customs, and being escorted into a waiting shuttle. Hazel was wide-eyed through it all, letting herself follow along behind Daniel like a child, relieved not to have to be the one to read the signs in the airport and decide which direction to go. It was all so much, so overstimulating, that it would have taken at least an hour longer if she had been on her own.

When she had told Daniel that, he had just shaken his head. "No, if you needed to figure things out, you would have. But since you have me here, you could relax. That's what friends are for, Craze. Next time, when you travel on your own, you can handle it all. I'm sure of it."

She had smiled back, had even appreciated his kind words, and had let the tired nickname slide. But she also knew that there would be such a long passage of time before this mythical "next time" that it was entirely possible the travel industry could undergo a major transformation. Daniel's job might have him traveling a lot, but a teacher's budget didn't exactly scream "international vacations every summer." To make things even worse, she doubted this little escape of theirs would be repeated any time soon. She would have loved to be Daniel's built-in plus one for all sorts of adventures, but considering how uncomfortable her feelings for him made things for both of them, it would be the surprise of the century if he invited her back again.

Plus, if he starts dating someone, there's no chance at all that she would be cool with you tagging along, she thought, her own mind surprising her. Why would she even want to join Daniel on a vacation with this hypothetical girlfriend of his? If that was where her mind went, to always assuming that she should be by his side even if the place was clearly occupied, then she was going to need to get her head on straight. She was going to need to remember that she could stand on her own two feet, that she didn't always need to be leaning up against him for support.

And that thought had followed her to the resort, where she had insisted on carrying her own bag, on not letting Daniel take her hand to help her down from the shuttle, on stepping out of his reach when he placed a hand on her lower back to steer her towards the reception desk. As easy as it was to fall into step beside him, she was resolved to do it at a bit of a distance, to take this time in this completely new place to let herself try on a different persona.

Would it perhaps be easier to reinvent herself if the great love of her life weren't sleeping in the same room as her? Probably. But Hazel was sure of one thing: no matter who she became in this life, and even if she and Daniel weren't meant to be, he was going to be a fixture in her reality. He was her best friend, and if she couldn't be all the different versions of herself contained within her being in front of him, then who *could* she be those people with?

"Everything okay?" he asked, shooting her a concerned expression while they waited for the receptionist to locate their reservation.

"Absolutely." She nodded. "I'm just figuring some stuff out. But it's going to be great."

"Is that Daniel Martin? Gosh, man, it's crazy to actually see you in person and not in a tiny Zoom box. Turns out you're fully three dimensional! Who would have guessed?" A man had approached them, clapping Daniel on the back and then shaking his hand.

Daniel turned to face the newcomer, a smile sliding into place on this face. "Oliver Wilson! And you aren't two inches tall! How's it going?"

As the two men chatted, Hazel sized them up, trying to read the unspoken dynamics between them. They looked to be about the same age, and she guessed from the jokes and the back slaps that they were employed at the same level—Daniel wouldn't be teasing his manager like that, would he? Where Daniel was blond and muscular, a former high school football player who liked to tell the story of how he scored the winning touchdown in Game 7, this newcomer—Oliver, Daniel had called him—looked more like the kind of nerdy guy that high school Daniel would have leaned on a little too hard to help him with his pre-calculus homework. Oliver was tall, broad shoulders tapering to a narrow waist, a pair of glasses perched on his nose.

He turned his attention to Hazel then, his already broad smile spreading impossibly wider. "And you must be—"

She cut in before he could assume the nature of their relationship. "I'm Hazel. Daniel's friend."

Was it her imagination or had his eyebrows twitched at that word? "Just a friend?" His eyes flicked quickly between the two of them, landing back on her with an intensity she couldn't understand.

She nodded. "Just a friend."

Oliver's eyes crinkled as his smile took on a new quality, his hand offered and accepted in Hazel's. "Happy to hear it. I, for one, am a huge fan of friends, and I have a sneaking suspicion that you and I should embark on a friendship of our own. What do you say, Hazel?"

Daniel blew out a sigh. "Craze, you don't—"

"I'd love that." She gave Oliver's hand an extra squeeze. "It's really nice to meet you, Oliver"

Four

"Okay, but, like...come *on*. Can't you see how weird it is for me for you to be friends with Oliver Wilson? I had never even met the guy in person before today, and, honestly, I'm not even sure if I like him. He's an accountant, for crying out loud. Who wants to be friends with an accountant?" As soon as Daniel had closed the door of their room behind him, he had set in on the interaction they had just had with Oliver.

Hazel took in the two queen-size beds in the room, pointing at the one closest to the window. "Can I take that one? Do you mind?"

"No, of course I don't mind. But can you please talk to me about Oliver? Are you really going to meet him for a walk by the sea? Do you not think that's a super weird thing to ask someone you just met?" He was leaning towards her, a strain in his expression she couldn't place.

And it wasn't as if he weren't justified in his discomfort. It *had* been a bit out of the blue when, as soon as Hazel had agreed to be Oliver's friend, fully expecting the interaction to end there, he had asked her—and *only* her, Daniel had been quick to point out—if she wanted to meet him back in the lobby in twenty minutes to go take a walk along the beach.

She must have looked confused, because Oliver had followed up immediately. "A bit of exercise is the best thing for getting over jet lag quickly, especially when the sun is still out and you're trying to acclimate to the new time zone. Also, I'm dying to do a bit of exploring, and I'd love the pleasure of your company. And finally, I promise I'm not a creep. Your friend Daniel can vouch for me and also for the fact that the Schuler Group has an explicit no creeps policy."

Hazel had chuckled at that. "I feel like you should have led with that. Because only now, after knowing that you aren't a creep, can I even consider your previous statements." She paused for a moment, taking a mental tally of all that he had said, while also noticing the humor dancing in his eyes. She heard a huffed sigh from behind her and felt Daniel's presence drawing closer. It was a physical reminder of her commitment to create space between them, to get over him as much as her heart would allow, and so she nodded at Oliver. "I would love to join you. Let me take my things to my room, and I'll be back in a flash."

Of course, in her room the quick transition she had imagined, where she would leave her bag to unpack later, change out of her travel clothes, and throw her hair into a butterfly clip, had been derailed. Daniel's attitude toward her impending meet-up with Oliver came out of nowhere and had her second guessing the entire thing.

"I think he just wants a friend," she said, opening her suitcase on the floor to look for a lighter jacket to replace the winter coat she had been wearing in New York. "Unlike you, he didn't bring one. And friendships aren't exactly exclusive relationships, Daniel. You're allowed to have more than one."

Daniel crossed his arms, leaning against the wardrobe across from her. "I know that. Of course I do. It just seems a bit juvenile to come right out and ask someone to be your friend like that. It's not like he and I are even friends."

She got back to her feet, jacket in hand. "And why is that? Do you think there's something wrong with Oliver? Some weird vibe you got? Some fatal flaw that makes him incapable of human friendship?" She tipped her head to the side, narrowing her eyes at Daniel. "Or is it just that you live in different cities and so going out for a beer has never been an option until now?" She sighed. "Why don't you come with us? Especially if the alternative option is sitting here by yourself and grumbling when there's a whole beautiful new world out there." She point towards the window, where a view of the Mediterranean Sea was waiting just beyond the curtains.

Daniel, like Scrooge himself, made a humphing sound. "He only invited you, Craze. I'm not crashing a party I wasn't invited to." He gestured towards the door. "Go, then. You don't want to keep your new friend waiting."

"You are ridiculous." Hazel grabbed the clothes she had extracted from her suitcase and stalked into the bathroom to change. "I just want to be clear that you are definitely also invited and so staying behind to pout is *definitely* a choice!" she called through the bathroom door.

"I can't hear you!" Daniel called back, the barest hint of laughter in his tone. "And even if I could, you're still wrong!"

She emerged from the bathroom a moment later, fully dressed, and held her hands out to her side. "If you genuinely don't want me to go…"

Daniel shook his head and smiled at her then, his earlier intensity falling away. "No, I was out of line. Oliver seems like a good dude, and he's definitely right about the Schuler Group's no creeps policy. You should have fun, and I could probably use a minute or two of peace and quiet. Might even grab a shower."

"Okay." She slipped one of the keys into her pocket and stepped towards the door. "See you later then."

Oliver was waiting in the lobby right where she had left him, and he gave her that dazzling grin again as she stepped off the elevator. "There she is, my new friend," he said, stepping towards her with his arms out, a gesture he seemed to think better of when patting her lightly on the arm rather than offering her a hug. "Are you ready to head out?"

She nodded back. "I am. I've been dying to stick my toes in the water since I got a glimpse of it out the window of the airplane."

"Me, too." He looked down at her, all childish wonder at the world awaiting them outside the resort. "I've been warned that it's going to be cold, but I'm refusing to listen to that. You don't come all the way to the Mediterranean Sea for the first time in your life just to look at it from a distance and call that good enough."

"I agree," said Hazel. "Daniel thought I was crazy for it, but that's nothing new for the two of us."

A hint of a frown wrinkled Oliver's forehead as he gestured towards the door, stepping aside to let Hazel exit first. "Is that why he calls you Craze?" he asked, pulling a face as their eyes made contact.

"Ah. You heard that," she said, rolling her eyes. "It's an old nickname, from all the way back in middle school when it was really clever and funny. I told him for a while that he should probably update it to something a little more age-appropriate, but I think it's just fossilized in his brain now. I don't mind it," she added quickly, not wanting to throw Daniel under the bus. "I just hope he remembers not to introduce me to his boss that way."

They made their way off the resort property, out onto the coastal road in front. Oliver gestured to the right and left in turn. "Which way should we go?"

Hazel looked both ways, noting that the left seemed to take them towards shops and restaurants while the right looked to be more hotels and then the open road beyond. The mountains were to the right as well, which sealed her decision. She pointed in that direction. "Always go towards the mountains. At least when the other option is souvenir shops." She nodded across the street. "Shouldn't we cross over and walk along the beach, though?"

"Absolutely." He crossed his arms over his chest and rubbed his upper arms against the cool breeze. "I'm not quite ready to dip my toes in the water yet, though."

"We'll warm up as we walk. Come on!" The light had just changed in the crosswalk, and Hazel grabbed Oliver's nearest wrist and towed him with her across the street.

"So, Hazel," said Oliver as they began to walk along the road above the beach. "Tell me about you. Who are you and what brings you here and…well, whatever else you feel like sharing?"

"There's not much to tell." She squinted at the sun that was beginning to dip towards the mountains, the warmth it left behind on her cheeks a welcome change from the gusts of cold wind she was accustomed to feeling in December. "I'm a teacher and it's Christmas break and Daniel invited me to tag along with him on this work trip. It's pretty cool that the Schuler Group lets people bring plus ones." She turned to study Oliver then. "Why didn't you bring someone? It seems like if it's a free thing, then there's no good reason not to." She narrowed her eyes at him. "Are you a repulsive human being? Couldn't find anyone who would agree to spend the time with you?" She shook her head. "That stinks. To be you, I mean."

He chuckled a little too loudly, shaking his head. "I had plans to bring someone, but things changed. And that's okay, that's why I'm now able to go on this walk with you, so I'd say it all turned out alright in the end."

It seemed like there was more that he wasn't saying, but Hazel didn't press the issue. "What about you? I told you about me, so that means it's your turn."

Oliver began to nod but then shook his head. "You don't get off the hook that easily. You told me the least interesting fact about yourself—your job—and then redirected back to me." He held up a hand. "I'm not saying I won't happily divulge my own story to you, but you've got to give me a little more than being a teacher tagging along on a free trip. What do you do for fun? Or why did it seem like a good idea to spend the holidays away from your normal people, assuming you normally celebrate a December holiday and normally spend it with some normal people?" He turned to study her expression. "Or are your people not normal?"

"I do normally spend the holidays—Christmas, to be specific, and New Year's too—with my family. Two parents and a brother. Jack, that's my brother's name. And he's great. I actually will really miss spending this time with them."

"...but? Why do I feel like there's a reason you aren't doing just that?"

Hazel sighed. "Well, that's a bit of a story, actually. Last Christmas, my brother got stranded in Munich and ended up meeting one of my favorite romance authors and starting a relationship with her."

Oliver widened his eyes at her. "My goodness. I can see why you wouldn't want to be around them. That sounds totally awful."

She elbowed him in his ribs, surprising herself with how comfortable she felt with a gesture like that. "Actually, it's not awful at all, and now they are two of my favorite people. Claire is the opposite of the whole 'never meet your heroes' thing. I decided last year that I was going to have a Christmas adventure of my own." She stopped herself from telling him that the original purpose she had intended for that adventure was to allow for the possibility of her own meet cute, her own happily ever after. Or that, the year before, Jack and Claire had been talking her through her most recent Daniel-related heartbreak. How could she explain that, when she was here, thousands of miles away from home, with the person she was supposed to be getting over?

"I see." Oliver nodded, silent as he processed her words. "That sounds like a great example to have in your life. And hey, I'm all for adventures. And why shouldn't one of them happen at Christmas time? I think that's part of the idea with the Schuler Group having us here now. They made the trip optional, and they let us bring along our families and plus ones. I know the resort gave them a great rate, but it's also, like...why shouldn't we leave our homes and do some exploring, just because it's Christmas?" He looked over at her. "Am I even making sense right now?"

Hazel slowly nodded. "I...think so? I mean, Christmas is one of the busiest travel times of the year, but I think that's mostly people traveling to be with their families. But you're right, traveling somewhere new, somewhere where people might even celebrate different holidays...that's nice, too." She held up a hand. "I'm not saying I'm going to make a habit of this. I will probably be only too ready to spend next year's Christmas break cuddled up on my parents' couch drinking hot chocolate. But for this year, at least, it's really nice to be here. I think. I mean, I barely even feel like I'm here yet, given that we just landed not even two hours ago." She shrugged. "I don't know. Somehow, it feels like it was the right choice."

Oliver's smile was small, with a hint of sadness at the corners. "I certainly hope so. I know how special it is to be with your loved ones, sharing your traditions. It's hard to adapt without them, but it doesn't mean you can't make new memories, can't still find something to love."

She wondered, not for the first time, why Oliver was alone and if it was the same reason that had turned his tone wistful, his gaze downcast. She wasn't going to pry. She barely knew him. If he wanted to tell her, he would.

They continued walking, now past the largest of the hotels. Oliver's hand landed on her elbow and he jerked his head towards the beach, where the waves were washing up on the empty shore, with not even one brave swimmer in sight. "It's time," he said, his voice the picture of serious resignation. "We must put our feet in the water."

Hazel clucked her tongue. "Well, I can't argue with a command like that. Come on, then." And she grabbed Oliver's hand in hers and steered him down the nearest set of stairs. They stopped at the bottom to slip off their shoes and socks, whooping with delight at the feel of cool sand underneath their feet.

"I don't know why I was still expecting hot sand," said Hazel as they made their way to the water's edge. "I suppose I should be grateful that it isn't cold enough to hurt my feet, at least."

"No," said Oliver, his strides growing longer and his smile growing broader the closer they came to the shore. "It's actually quite pleasant. If the water is anything like the sand, then I just might have to come back later with my swim trunks—"

His sentence cut off as he stepped onto the small wet rocks at the water's edge, a wave crashing into shore that reached up to his ankles. Hazel, who had been slightly less eager to touch the water, threw her head back in laughter from where she stood on the dry sand.

"Changing your mind?" she asked. "A little colder than you expected?"

But if she had forgotten that she was still holding Oliver's hand, he hadn't. He tugged gently on her hand then, pulling her towards the water as she resisted, self-preservation instincts on high as if the sea were made of lava. It was a quick tug-of-war, though, with Oliver's grip steady but gentle, not so firm that she couldn't easily escape if she had wanted to, as he watched her dance around him with laughter in his eyes.

Hazel was almost free, almost grounded enough in her footing to be able to give her wrist one good tug and escape the sea's icy grip when an errant stone threw her off her footing. She stumbled, careening towards the sand, the picture of what happens when gracefulness leaves the room or when it may never have been there to begin with.

Oliver reacted quickly, pulling her towards himself and wrapping his arms around her to steady her. It was only when she realized that, rather than bruising her knees falling onto the rocks, she was encased in warmth, protected from the wind by Oliver's looming presence and held steady by his arms, only when she took a full inventory of her unscathed state that she realized where she was standing.

"It's freezing!" she cried, the water churning over her ankles. She felt Oliver's chest quake with silent laughter as she pounded halfheartedly on his solid chest. "I can't believe you made me get in the water with you."

"You mean you can't believe I stopped you from face-planting on the beach?" She felt his voice rumbling under her ear as much as she heard it, and an accompanying jolt of electricity traveled up her spine. "You're welcome, Hazel. That's what friends are for."

Five

"Once your feet go numb, it's actually really nice," said Hazel, still planted firmly where the shallowest waves broke on the shore.

"Come on out a little deeper then." Oliver squeezed her hand, an unspoken alliance to stay physically linked, holding firm after Hazel's near tumble on the beach. Oliver had waded out slightly deeper, but only as far as the hands tethering them together would allow.

Hazel shook her head. "I'm good. I'm happy with my feet being numb, but I can't say the same for my ankles." She let go of his hand, though his grip held firm, keeping them connected. "You go on ahead, though." She tipped her head back towards the beach. "I'll go sit and watch. I'll be your lifeguard, but if you have a problem, I can't promise to make it out to you in time. The water *is* very cold, and while I'm sure your impending crisis will motivate me to move more quickly, I can't guarantee I'll make it there in time to fight off a shark or ask the jellyfish to leave you alone."

"I haven't seen any sharks or jellyfish, so I think we'll be good." He walked back towards her. "Let's go sit and look at the sea, dry off our feet before we head back."

"You can go out farther," said Hazel. "I don't want to keep you from your fun."

He squeezed her hand, his eyes warm on hers, a stark contrast to the water lapping at her toes. "You couldn't possibly. All of this is fun. It's actually more fun hanging out with you than giving my calves an ice bath."

"The highest of praise," she replied, but she couldn't help but smile. They made their way to some large, smooth rocks that were catching the last of the day's sun, warm to the touch from the rays, and sat down side by side, finally releasing their grip on each other. "Oh, and thanks for not dragging me into the water against my will. That was very cool of you. The epitome of gentlemanly behavior."

Oliver turned slowly to look at her, a frown creasing his forehead. "You're...welcome? Would you also like to thank me for not pulling your hair and tripping you on the stairs? I have some questions about your standards for human behavior if you think not shoving someone into cold water against their will is worth celebrating."

She laughed, but her cheeks were heating, too. "I just meant...well, sometimes friendships get a little playful, and sometimes it isn't entirely clear where the line is."

He raised his eyebrows. "Oh, no. It was perfectly clear where the line was, when you said you didn't want to come farther out into the water. I wouldn't have made you touch it at all, but it was sort of unavoidable when I caught you from tripping." Oliver's eyes widened as he looked out into the distance, searching for the horizon beyond the blue expanse of water. "I don't think I've thought a girl saying, 'no, stop,' was just a cute thing girls say when they're having fun since I was about seven years old and kept tickling my little sister until she peed. Grandma gave me a good talking to after that one, and if there's one thing I hold to as a standard for living a good life, it's behaving in such a way that she would never have to do that again." He shivered at the memory. "I mean, I still regret that one foray into bullying my little sister, and it's been...a minute."

"About fifty years?" Hazel offered, trying to bring the light-hearted tone that had vanished when Oliver started reminiscing about childhood misadventures. "Back in the good old days?"

He rolled his eyes. "Yes, that's right. It was back in the day before we had cars. We traveled around in a horse and buggy. Not like the kids these days." He leaned a shoulder against hers, just for a second. "No, it *was* in the previous century, but more like the 1990s, not the 1900s. Surely you remember what the 90s were like with their 'boys will be boys' excuses. Of course, thankfully, Grandma didn't subscribe to any of that."

"Was that really just a 'thing' in the previous century?" Hazel bit her lower lip. "Because I might have to tell Daniel. Oh, I'm sure he's a perfect gentleman in his romantic relationships, but damn if he doesn't miss a chance to mess with me."

Oliver leaned towards her, his eyes not leaving hers. "Oh, you're going to have to elaborate. Because if Daniel and I need to have a talk..."

"No, it's not like that." She put a hand on his forearm, nodding. "Really, I swear. It's more just like the sort of dumb stuff we did when we first met, which was when we were twelve. Maybe it's hard to outgrow who you were at the beginning of your friendship. But he would definitely have tugged me into the water with him today." She winced. "No, that's not true. He would have pushed me in ahead of him. He *might* have asked if my phone was in my pocket first, so at least it didn't get ruined. But that's really hit or miss."

Oliver blinked slowly. "You're serious? I mean, I'm fairly sure that you *are* serious, but if you'd like to take this opportunity to set me straight, that would be great. And if you don't, then I think Daniel and I really are going to have to have a word. You know that isn't okay, right?"

Hazel sighed. "It sounds so much worse than it actually is, Oliver. We're friends. I think he sees me more like a little sister than a friend, even."

"I will point to Exhibit A again of my treatment of my own sister and subsequent chastisement from my grandmother to remind you that that doesn't make it okay." He studied her face. "Why do you put up with it? You seem like a woman who doesn't have a hard time expressing herself or asking for what she wants. You told me you didn't want to go in the water. Don't you do the same with Daniel?"

"It's...different, I guess." Her cheeks felt like they were burning under the gaze of both Oliver and the sun. "I love our friendship. It's one of my favorite things in life. I don't want to mess it up by suddenly changing the rules. And it's not like Daniel ever takes things too far or anything like that. If anything, he's always telling me what a good sport I am, how he doesn't get to be himself like that with anyone else."

"Well, if 'himself' is someone who likes to disrespect boundaries and act like a jerk, then maybe he should try being himself a little less." Oliver licked his lip, his eyes drifting to the sea and then back. "You have feelings for him?"

Hazel blew out a surprised sigh. "Is it that obvious?" She hadn't exactly intended to make Oliver her confidant or to take on the identity of 'Daniel's tag along friend who's in love with him' to anyone on this trip. And yet, it was so easy to talk to Oliver, so natural to let her response to his question tumble from her lips. "I do," she said. "And I think I see what you're getting at. You think I let him behave however he wants to because I want him to see that I'm different, that I'm the only one he can really be himself with, and that it means that we're meant to be together." She sniffed out a laugh. "And you may not be wrong about that. I mean, I do get frustrated with his childish behavior sometimes, but I stop myself from saying something."

"Why? Why wouldn't you speak up?"

She shrugged. "It's a couple different things. I don't know if I'm frustrated with him as a friend or if I'm frustrated as someone who loves him, who wants to be with him. And you aren't supposed to start nagging someone before you're even in a relationship with them, I'm pretty sure. Plus, it's entirely possible that he does these sorts of things to keep me squarely in the friend zone. Especially since I may have made it a little too clear to him that I wanted to exit that particular zone."

Oliver's eyes widened almost imperceptibly. "He knows how you feel?"

Hazel nodded. "He does."

"And I take it he doesn't feel the same way?"

"He does not."

One small, humorless laugh escaped from Oliver's lips. "Man, I will never understand the human heart. So, the two of you are on different pages—or maybe even reading entirely different books, actually—about your relationship, and yet you're still good friends. And not just good friends, but the sort of friends who spend Christmas together on vacation in another country."

"I..." What was the point of sharing from her heart if she wasn't going to lay it all out on the line? "It's not exactly new territory for us. I've confessed my feelings for him more than once, either because I'm a glutton for punishment or because I'm actually convinced that someday he's going to see things differently and I don't want to miss that when it comes around." She pressed her lips together. "Actually, though, today was the first time in a long time that I thought maybe I should try to let it all go. That I could just focus on being me and on being happy and healthy and not hung up on someone who's just never going to feel differently about me."

Oliver was focused on the horizon then, giving her the space to feel her feelings without the scrutiny of his gaze. "Do you really believe that? That he's never going to change the way he feels?" He glanced over at her then, just briefly. "Or is it one of those tricks where you try to convince yourself you don't want something in order to trick life into giving you exactly that thing?"

She had to laugh at that. "Well, today it felt genuine. But I can't tell you what it's going to be like tomorrow." She poked him softly in the side, making him jolt. "It really did help talking about all of this with you. It's hard to say out loud that my dream guy would have pushed me into the frigid sea while letting him maintain that particular title. And the more you react to the bad behavior I've been tolerating, the harder it is to tell myself that it's okay."

Oliver smiled at her then. "I'm happy to provide the service. And if you need it again at any time, you know where to find me. I'm more than happy to be your friend, and in particular the sort of friend who doesn't push you into traffic or try to keep you as one of my bros, reminding you constantly that you don't even qualify as a member of the potential dating pool..." He turned his eyes skyward and took a beat. "Sorry. Got carried away. I'm happy to be your friend, and I'm sure Daniel is too, in his own way."

"He's a good guy, really." Hazel sighed. "It's dawning on me right now just how messed up it was to air his dirty laundry to one of his colleagues. Please don't let my experience with Daniel—in particular just this facet of my experience with him, since we have a lot more history than just my little unrequited crush...don't let this one aspect of him color what you think of him as a colleague, as a person. He's a good guy, and he's good at his job."

"Don't worry about a thing, Hazel. For one thing, your secrets are safe with me. And for another thing, I already liked Daniel. We may have never met in person, but we always had a laugh together on our virtual meetings and I had the feeling he was someone I could trust to hold his end of a bargain and also someone I'd like to have a beer with in person."

Hazel clapped her hands. "That's it! We should do that!"

"Do...what?"

"We should all have dinner together tonight. You and Daniel will finally get to spend some time getting to know each other, and I won't have to keep myself up until all hours worrying that I over shared, that I said something I shouldn't have. You two will have a nice time together, and once I see that I didn't break that, then maybe I can let go of this sneaking feeling I'm having that the particular combination of jet lag, cold ankles, and those big brown eyes of yours worked like a truth serum to make me spill my guts."

Oliver gave her an exaggerated blink, widening his eyes. "These bad boys? They're my secret weapons. Though I mostly used them as a kid to convince my grandma that a scoop of ice cream wouldn't ruin my dinner. I can't help it if she believed me every time, even with zero evidence to this day to back it up."

"That's the second time you've mentioned your grandmother," said Hazel. "It seems like she was a bit of a fixture in your childhood, at least based on my tiny sampling of data."

Oliver smiled, a wistfulness in his eyes that wasn't there before. "She was, yeah. She's...she was the best. Definitely a starring role in most of my favorite memories."

"Is she still...?" How did you ask a question like that? Hazel wanted to kick herself as soon as the words came out, cementing her status as a failure in all the social graces. Not only had she spilled her deepest secret, but now she was asking Oliver about the health and wellness and mortality of his nearest and dearest? *Now would be the perfect time for a portal to another world to open up and just vanish me entirely from this one.*

"No, she passed away." Oliver cleared his throat, pushing up the corners of his mouth as if reassuring her that it was okay for them to talk about this. "Not that long ago, actually."

"Oh, I'm so sorry." She reached for him, stopped herself, wondering if it was appropriate, and then reached again, her hands coming around his shoulders as she pressed him to herself. "That must be just awful. I'm sorry for prying into your life, and I'm even more sorry that you lost such a wonderful person."

Oliver was quiet for a moment, his own hand hesitant when it finally found a place to rest on her back. When he spoke again, his voice was quiet, more of a vibration under her ear, something she felt, than something she heard. "Thank you, Hazel. But don't be sorry for prying. I wouldn't have brought up Grandma so many times if I didn't want to talk about her. I miss her a lot and I'm thinking about her constantly, so it makes sense that I would find any excuse under the sun to bring her up. And it feels better to talk about her than to not talk about her."

"You can talk about her to me anytime." Hazel gave him one more squeeze, then forced herself to release her grip and take a step back. "I mean it, Oliver. If you're feeling sad, missing your grandma, or if you just want to reminisce about the good old days, I'm your gal. I'll be your emotional plus one. It seems like you already agreed to be mine, so it only makes sense to return the favor."

A shadow crossed his features. "You don't have to do something in return just because you shared something with me."

"I know. But as it turns out, I like talking to you, and everything I've heard about your grandma so far—teaching a young man about consent *and* eating ice cream for dinner? She sounds like my hero!—makes me think I would have really liked her. You'll be doing me a favor if you share a little bit more of her with me."

"Thank you, Hazel. Really." Oliver pulled her towards him for one more quick embrace before straightening back to his full height and tipping his head towards the hotel. "Let's get back then. Time to collect our favorite Daniel Martin and take him to dinner."

Six

"**G**ood, you're back," said Daniel when Hazel slipped into the hotel room. He was propped against the headboard of his bed, novel in hand. "I was about to come looking for you. Thought maybe you two got lost or something." He set his book down on the nightstand, his smile thin and his eyes tired. "Did you and Oliver have fun? I don't know him well, so I hope he wasn't a giant nerd."

Hazel slipped off her shoes and went into the bathroom to rinse off her feet in the tub. "That's such a weird insult, dude. I mean, seriously." She called back to him over the sound of the running water. "Maybe it was okay for the jocks to pick on the nerds in, like, the 80s and 90s, but by now surely we must admit that nerds have got it going on. They've got the sort of skills that will keep them fed and watered for life, and the rest of us should be more like them." She turned off the water, patting her feet dry on the bath mat before heading out to sit on her bed, facing Daniel. "But we had a good time. Oliver seems to have solid friend potential, and it'll be good for me—and for you—if I have another one of those while we're here. You'll surely want to get me out of your hair from time to time, and I need to look at someone else's face every so often."

Daniel scoffed. "Yeah, right. Like you could ever get sick of looking at my face."

If only he knew how true that is, she thought before reminding herself that he did, in fact, know how true that was. "Absence makes the heart grow fonder, bud."

"In that case, I should probably never let you out of my sight. It might help you move on from your little crush." Daniel winced. "Sorry. I heard it as soon as I said it. That wasn't very kind and compassionate of me, now was it?" He scooted closer, still out of arm's reach. "I really don't want to be a jerk, Craze. I know it's a little strange, our whole situation, but I don't want to lose you as a friend. I want us to be able to joke about things, you know? To be normal? But I don't know how to joke about you having feelings for me without it seeming like I don't take you seriously. And I do take you seriously, of course I do."

"Then can I make a suggestion?" When he nodded, she continued. "Maybe let's just not talk about the whole crush thing. For you, joking about it is supposed to take away some of its power. But for me, joking about it feels like getting fresh stabs in the heart every time, reminding me that I wanted something I have no chance of ever getting. And as much as I normally like talking about anything and everything, leaving no conversational stone unturned...I think I'd really like to leave this one alone."

"Really?" He narrowed his eyes at her. "What happened out there with Oliver? Is he a wizard? Did he transform some fundamental aspect of your personality? How can I get the old Hazel back?"

"It's not about Oliver." Well, maybe it was a *little* about Oliver, especially if he was going to be her confidant for the next two weeks. "It's about the fact that I normally talk to you about everything, right? We work through all my problems and frustrations together, and you're one of my favorite people to pick through tricky topics with." She bit her lower lip. "The problem is that the particular tricky topic I need to work through is...well, you. And I don't think it can possibly be a good idea to try to work through that together. It's like asking the Easter Bunny to help me stop eating sugar. Or trying to stop drinking by taking a tour of wine country. Does that make sense?"

Daniel nodded slowly. "It...does, I guess. I'm not crazy about being compared with an addictive substance, though I suppose that could be considered a compliment in some sort of twisted way." His gaze bounced between her eyes, searching for something. "And I really like being your best friend, being the one who helps you untangle your strings. Don't use this to pull away from me, okay? We can still find plenty of other things to talk about, even if we leave this one topic alone."

Hazel laughed at that. "I can promise I will still have plenty of strings that need to be untangled. If, for example, you would like to help me come up with my lesson plans for the first week of classes, that would be much appreciated. And I'm sure there will be other things that come up as time goes on. I solemnly resolve not to have all my shit together just because we stop talking about one particular topic. Sound good?"

"Sounds great." His smile was relieved, his shoulders dropping slightly as he shifted in his seat. "So what should we get up to tonight? It's our first night in Turkey, and I was looking at some restaurant suggestions on my phone..."

"Oh, right! I forgot to tell you." Hazel sat up a little straighter. "We're going to meet up with Oliver for dinner. I mean, that doesn't put a damper on any of your plans because we hadn't actually talked about restaurants or anything. We just decided that it would be nice for the three of us to eat together. Does that sound good to you?"

Daniel frowned. "I thought it would just be the two of us. I mean, the work retreat part of this thing hasn't really started yet, but I imagine when it does, we'll have some required evening activities and meals to attend. For tonight, at least, I imagined just us." He sighed. "But you guys already decided on this, right? If I change the plans now, he's going to know I was the one who didn't want him to tag along."

"Technically, you're the one who's tagging along." Hazel raised an eyebrow at Daniel, a challenge if she'd ever given one. "Since it was Oliver and me who made this plan in the first place. And not to bring up the same topic we've just resolved not to discuss, but perhaps avoiding putting ourselves in too many situations that could have us mistaken for a couple wouldn't be the worst idea we've ever had."

"I wasn't—"

She held up a hand. "I know you didn't mean it that way. And maybe it's just my sharp intuitive skills at work—or maybe it's just the most predictable thing about male-female friendships—but I know that if we're sitting at a table together and one of your coworkers sees you there, it's only a matter of seconds before they're going to be asking to be introduced to your wife or girlfriend." She sniffed. "And it doesn't end there. Even if you tell them that I'm your friend, there are still going to be meaningful looks exchanged and scoffing tones. This isn't my first trip around that particular block, Daniel."

He looked at her as if he was seeing her for the first time. "This has happened before? But...when?"

"You wouldn't have noticed it because it wouldn't have meant anything to you. But to me, harboring my secret crush on you in the days before I told you, I took every single one of those interactions as some kind of sign that we were meant to be together. A waitress at a Waffle House thinks we're a cute couple? Great, file that away for a speech at our wedding. Your college roommate winks at me when you aren't looking, right after you've introduced me as your best friend? Well, clearly, that means he knows your true feelings and will be delivering another speech at that aforementioned wedding. I filed all of it away."

Daniel blinked. "That's...intense."

Something inside Hazel snapped. "No, not really. That's just being a woman in a world that's obsessed with pairing us off with men. In a world that loves to tell you the secret to a happy life is marrying your best friend. A world that is so sure women and men can't be friends that there are entire genres of movies revolving around that truth. All of it, all of that messaging I've been consuming since even before I met you, all of it came together to add this extra layer of *significance* to every damn thing." She sighed.

"And I'm so tired of it. It hasn't been good for me, and it hasn't been good for us. So can we just…"

"Eat dinner with Oliver?" Daniel offered, when her sentence trailed off. His smile was gentle, even if his eyes had a shell-shocked look to them.

She barked out a laugh despite herself. "Well, that's a good start. So yeah. I was going to ask if we could just be normal, and that's a step in the right direction. Plus, I mean…Oliver seems like a cool and normal human who will be nice to be around. Not that he exists just to be a buffer between us in this weird uncharted friendship territory of ours."

"Of course not. We'll keep him around for his quick wit and superior intellect, not for his unique ability to remove any hint of possible mistaken romantic vibes."

She frowned at him. "That's a bit harsh. I'm sure Oliver doesn't automatically cause any romantic vibes to evaporate like magic. In the right circumstances, I bet he can even amplify or create them."

Daniel nodded. "Sure. I just hope I don't have to see him do that."

Oliver met them in the lobby an hour later. The three of them had decided via group text—Hazel had been quick to create it as soon as Daniel had agreed to the dinner—to forgo the resort's restaurant that evening for a fish restaurant a short walk down the road.

"Good to see you again, man," said Daniel, pulling Oliver in to transform their handshake into a mutual slap on the back. "And thanks for showing Hazel around earlier."

Oliver gave Daniel a smile, then released his hand to pull Hazel in for a quick embrace. "It was my absolute pleasure. Hello again, Hazel. You look lovely."

"Thank you," she replied, feeling her cheeks heat at the attention. In the previous hour, she had showered and thrown on a deep teal dress she had found in her suitcase, not something fancy enough to warrant a compliment like Oliver's, but still something that made her feel nice, in one of her favorite colors. She raised her eyebrows as she flashed him a quick smile. "Shall we head out, then?"

"Absolutely." He held out a hand, gesturing for her to go ahead and lead the way.

Daniel fell into step beside her, closer than normal, something almost possessive in his bearing. Oliver let the two of them exit together, then joined them on the sidewalk, joining Hazel on her other side. As the three of them began the short walk to the restaurant, she wondered for the first time if it was a mistake for them to think they could all enjoy an evening out together. If it were just her and Daniel, she knew they could entertain themselves just fine. She and Oliver had proven they could do the same just an hour before. The question, she supposed, was if the two men could enjoy each other's company or if there was some unique alchemy created by the combination of all three of them that was making everything feel so awkward.

"So...guys," she began, a jolt of nervous laughter surprising her. "This is your first time hanging out, so...uh...what do you want to talk about? What do you normally talk about for small talk at your work meetings? Sports? The weather?" She looked to the sea, the earlier waves calmed down in the early evening hour, its surface now as smooth as glass. "The weather here is pretty great, isn't it? Better than New York for sure, and probably better than wherever Oliver is from, too."

"Detroit," said Oliver and Daniel together.

"Right," said Hazel. "Was I right, then? What's the weather like this time of year in Detroit?"

"Oh, it's probably not that different from New York. Colder than here, that's for sure. We haven't had our first snow of the season yet, but I expect it will come soon." He grimaced then. "God, Hazel, you really did get us to talk about the weather." He looked over at Daniel, reaching a hand over to give him a good natured tap on the arm. "Come on, man, I'm sure we can find more things in common to talk about than the basic human experience of living on a planet that has weather."

Daniel smiled and nodded. "I'm sure you're right. And in order to not subject Hazel to the worst kind of torture, let's resolve now to not talk about work. Deal?"

"Deal. What are you looking forward to doing while we're here in Turkey? Got any big plans for the upcoming days?"

"Oh, definitely." Daniel's eyes had brightened with the question. "I've heard there's some great hiking around here, and lots of ancient sites to check out. It's my first time traveling in this part of the world, and I'm planning to make the most of it. Of course, there will probably be some work obligations, committee meetings and such, getting in the way of that. But essentially, I don't want to waste a single free moment."

Oliver gave him a thoughtful nod. "I hear you. Yeah, it definitely makes sense to try to make the most of it. I think I want to get up to a fraction of what you're talking about. I mean, I definitely don't want to miss the chance to sit in the ruins of an amphitheater and imagine who else might have sat there centuries before." His smile was sheepish. "But I'm also going to do some resting while I'm here, too. I brought a few books with me, and I see nothing wrong with finding a nice cafe with a view of the sea and losing track of time there."

"Yes, please!" Hazel cut in with a nod. "I'm inviting myself along for that. Like, I definitely want to do some hiking with Daniel, but I also forgive you, Daniel"—she turned to face her friend—"for being so overly enthusiastic and optimistic with your travel plans. Luckily for you, though, it sounds like Oliver will be able to babysit me while you do your twelfth hike of the week." She turned to Oliver then. "Right? I assumed, but I didn't actually check—"

"Right." His smile was warm. "I'm more than happy to have your company any day of the week."

"Thank you. I've got reading to do, too." She didn't even want to think about the stack of history tests she had stashed in her carry-on to grade over the Christmas break. "An early copy of my future sister-in-law's new novel sounds like the perfect thing to enjoy with a little hot chocolate and the sound of gentle waves in the distance."

"Okay, guys." Daniel had picked up his pace and was looking back at them to keep up. "Let's hustle a bit. I want to beat the dinner rush at the restaurant."

Hazel and Oliver exchanged a glance before she let her eyes drift away, some disloyal feeling creeping over her at the secret smile that had formed on her lips. Instead, she crossed her purse strap over her chest and began to power walk to keep up with her old friend.

Seven

As it turned out, their hurry to reach the restaurant
had been unnecessary. They were greeted at the door
by smiling wait staff who looked only too surprised to have
dinner guests arrive. It would only become clear as the dinner wore on, when their dessert dishes were being cleared
as a line stretched out the door, that they had simply been
a bit earlier than most of the restaurant's regular patrons.

Because of their early arrival, though, they had gotten
their choice of prime seats for their meal, opting for a small
table on the top floor with a full view of the sunset over the
sea, just across the street. Daniel and Oliver had stepped
to opposite sides of the table, both of them standing back
to leave space for Hazel to slide in beside them. Her eyes
had darted between the two men, between Daniel's raised
eyebrow and Oliver's smirk, before she had steered herself
towards the chair next to Daniel. It might have been her
imagination, but it seemed like he stood just a little taller
as she walked towards him.

Of course, as soon as she sat down, a problem presented
itself. Her chair must have had three legs that were one

length and one that was just half an inch shorter because with every movement she was wobbling back and forth. Hazel tried to sit perfectly still, to not attract any attention to her predicament, but as she tightened her core muscles to stay perfectly upright while she reached for the water glass Oliver was offering her, he cleared his throat.

"Is there a problem with your chair?" he asked. Once she had taken the glass, he reached for the chair next to him, testing its legs and finding them sturdy. "Come sit here. This one doesn't wobble at all."

"You can switch the chairs," said Daniel, reaching towards Oliver as if he were going to lift the heavy chair over the table as the two of them sat.

"It's fine." Hazel got to her feet, retrieved her purse, and hurried to the empty seat next to Oliver. "I can sit here."

"I didn't say you couldn't. I just thought that since you *chose* to sit here that you might like the view from this seat a little more." Oh gosh, was Daniel pouting?

Hazel shook her head. "All of the views are great." She gestured towards the window. "It's really an incredible location, isn't it?"

"It is," Oliver agreed, and Daniel nodded, too. "What should we order? What are you both feeling up for?"

Hazel picked up the menu in front of her and began flipping pages. "I am realizing only as I look at this just how much knowledge about fish I lack. I mean, I don't know the difference between sea bass and sea bream, so I don't think I'm going to be much help." She looked across the table at her old friend, asking for help with her eyes. "Do you know what to order?"

"I generally like swordfish," he said, giving her a smile, "but I don't know that any of us really need to commit wholeheartedly to any one thing on the menu."

"That's a great idea," said Oliver, turning back to an earlier page in the menu. "We could order a variety of the different meze dishes and share them. Mostly hot dishes, maybe a few cold ones, too. That way, we can all taste as much of the menu as possible."

"That sounds great," said Hazel, exhaling a small sigh of relief. Menu anxiety was a real thing, she knew only too well. More often than not, she would order the first thing that appealed to her at a new restaurant, only to be carried away by the despair of smelling someone else's food and knowing that she had made the wrong choice. Tonight, though, that would not be the case. She closed her menu and leaned back against her chair. "I trust you both to make the right choices. Daniel, you know what I like."

Daniel wrinkled his nose. "You can't pressure me like that, Craze. What if I order all the wrong stuff and then you blame it on me?" He pushed her menu back towards her. "Take a look at it. Come on."

Oliver chanced a glance at her over his menu. "What exactly is it that you don't like, Hazel? I'm up for the challenge of trying to help you decide. And I like to think my ego isn't so delicate that it couldn't handle a little constructive criticism about my menu selections."

"Dude." Daniel was looking at Oliver with something like contempt. "There's nothing wrong with me and Craze and the way we do things. She doesn't need to be babied, doesn't need me to read a freaking menu for her. We're adults and we've been friends for a lot longer than you've known either one of us, so maybe could you stop trying to make me look like a bad guy by fawning over my friend?"

"Daniel." Hazel spoke through gritted teeth. "It isn't Oliver that is making everything weird and tense right now. Will you cut it out?" She glanced around the seating area, finding it still mercifully empty. "Just because we're alone up here doesn't mean you should act like we're just friends hanging out, watching the game and giving each other shit."

"Craze, this isn't between me and you. This is between me and him."

Oliver held up a hand, redirecting Daniel's attention back to himself from Hazel. "May I ask why you keep calling Hazel Craze? It doesn't seem like a particularly affectionate or kind nickname for such a lovely person."

"It's an inside joke. A long story." Daniel was shooting daggers at Oliver with his eyes now. "And I don't want to get into it right now." He gestured to the menu. "Will you just decide what you want to order? I'm starving, and this conversation is pissing me off."

Oliver glanced at Hazel, a slight nod to check that she was okay, and then they all resumed looking at their menus. They lapsed into silence until their waiter returned to take their order, all of them suggesting different small dishes to share—a salad and crab ordered by Hazel, mussels and calamari by Oliver, and a couple of different fish by Daniel.

When the waiter left, Daniel took a sip of his water and cleared his throat. "I'm sorry, guys," he said, his gaze directed solely at Hazel. "I think I'm like something out of one of those Snickers commercials, totally losing control of myself just because I'm hungry." He darted a quick glance at Oliver, an involuntary swallow at the same time. "I'll behave now that we're about to eat."

"It's fine," said Hazel, nudging his foot with hers under the table. "I'm used to it. I should have warned Oliver that you were likely to get hangry. He's the one who didn't know what he was getting into by agreeing to a meal with us."

The silence between them was more comfortable then, but it wasn't long before Daniel excused himself to find the restroom. Oliver turned to Hazel when they were alone, blinking at her slowly.

"What's on your mind?" she asked, taking a sip of water with practiced nonchalance. "You look like you need to get something off your chest."

"Hmm." He nodded. "Yeah, that might be. I just...I can't say I understand the two of you, not exactly. I get that you're old friends. That part makes sense to me."

"So what part is it that doesn't make sense to you?"

Oliver traced the condensation on his water glass. "I don't understand the way you let him talk to you, treat you...and especially not that you put up with all of that nonsense and still hold on to hope that the two of you could be a couple some day."

Hazel blinked. "Wow, tell me how you really feel."

"I'm not trying to be hurtful, Hazel." Oliver placed a light touch on her wrist before removing his hand back to the table. "I just don't think a man who talks over you, who thinks it's funny to call you by a nickname that implies you're crazy—I assume that's the *long story* about your nickname that he didn't want to get into…how is a man like that ever going to be a man who cherishes you and treats you the way you so clearly deserve to be treated?"

"You're missing the point, clearly." She spoke through gritted teeth. "Some of us aren't looking for the fairy tale we've been sold by books and movies our entire lives. I don't need someone who pulls out chairs and holds doors open and protects me from things like having to stand up for myself or make a decision or do basic math. I'm looking for someone who feels like home and comfort and the safest, softest place to land."

Oliver nodded. "I understand all of that. So does being called Craze feel like home and comfort and a safe, soft place to land?"

Hazel shrugged. "I guess so. It must, right? Because Daniel definitely does feel like all of those things. I know he isn't perfect, but he's a fixture in my life and I can't imagine it without him."

Oliver was silent for a beat, shadows passing across his eyes. "I would never suggest that Daniel shouldn't be in your life. Friends, family, the people who feel like home…we should treasure them." He looked at her then, an intensity in his eyes that she hadn't seen yet that day. "I am only suggesting that, when it comes to what you deserve in a romantic partner, you consider raising your standards. You may not think you need to be treated like a princess, but I don't think you would go wrong with a higher standard of respect and kindness. That's all."

"Daniel does respect me, and he is kind to me. You're just seeing a different side of him tonight."

Oliver's nod was thoughtful, considered. "And why is that? Is it really this bullshit about him being hungry? What kind of grown adult regresses to basic toddler behavior just because his tummy is a little hungry?" He leaned back in his chair and crossed his arms over his chest. "Or is it about me being here? About me treating you differently than he does and him...I don't know...peacocking?"

Hazel had to laugh at that. "I don't think Daniel is peacocking. For one thing, I'm not even entirely sure what that means. But for another thing, he doesn't see you as a threat. He might just be reacting to you not really getting him. Not really getting us and the way we are together."

"Hmm." Oliver nodded again. "That could be true. It doesn't change anything for me, though, in terms of my interpretation of the evening. Daniel is a fine colleague and I'm sure he's a good friend. You, though..." He gave her a sincere smile. "It's not even princess treatment you deserve, Hazel. You should be treated like a queen."

Hazel gagged, though it was at least in part in an effort to hide the effect his words were having on her. "Your concerns are duly noted, sir. Now please, let's move on from this before Daniel comes back to the table. The last thing I need is him walking up when you're saying something cheesy like that."

"That's fair enough." He leaned back, holding up his hands in surrender. "I'll behave. Keep my cheesiness to myself."

Hazel straightened her silverware on the table, still not willing to look at Oliver. "See that you do, please."

By the time they left the restaurant, all three of them practically needed to be rolled back to the hotel. If the small plates they had ordered had truly looked small at the beginning, by the time they had eaten every last morsel, from the second round of dishes they had ordered before even finishing the first round to the two different desserts that they had split three ways, they were all stuffed to the gills—pun intended.

"Oh my gosh, I should have stopped before the cheese-cake." Hazel clutched her stomach outside the restaurant, rubbing her swollen belly in apology. "Oh, who am I kidding? That was never going to happen. Every single thing in there was so delicious, there was zero chance of me practicing any moderation."

"Same here." Daniel was patting his stomach beside her. "I think I need to go for a longer walk now or else I'm going to be up all night, burping fish and having acid reflux."

Hazel winced. "Too much information, dude. Didn't need to know that." She shot Oliver a glance. "Are you a health nut too, or are you going to come back to the hotel with me?"

"I like a good walk as much as the next guy," said Oliver, "but I choose you." He smiled at her, the edges of his lips loosened by the bottle of wine the three of them had shared. He held out a hand for Daniel, the two of them clasping their palms together as some unspoken communication passed between them. "Be safe out there in the world, dude. I'll make sure your friend gets back home safely."

"You're good, Craze? I mean, Haze?" Daniel asked, his brow raised in anticipation of her answer.

She nodded at him. "Totally. I'm just ready to get home and crash for the night. I might call Jack first, just to let him and everyone know how things are going here."

"Say hi to them all for me," said Daniel, pulling her in for a quick hug. "You've got your key, right? I've got mine, so if you fall asleep before I get back, I'll slip in without waking you up."

"Good," she said. "And remember that my bed is the one by the window. I don't need you jostling into the bed beside me by mistake. That's how people end up getting punched, and you don't want to have a black eye on the first day of your work party."

"It's not a party," said Daniel, and Oliver was beside him, nodding in agreement.

"Well, whatever it is," said Hazel, "you still don't want to have to explain why your non-romantic plus one punched you in the face. So stay in your own bed, and we won't have any problems."

"I can agree to that," said Daniel. "Have a good night, you two. Get back safe, and get some rest."

Once they were out of reach of the restaurant's lights, Oliver bumped softly into Hazel's side, catching her around her elbow when she started to lose her balance. "Sorry," he said, laughing at himself. "That was just supposed to be a hip check, a way to ask you how you're doing without having to use actual words."

She laughed back. "But you forgot that, thanks to the power of both jet lag and wine, my ability to stay upright might not be as solid as it once was." She put her fingers over his hand that was still cradling her elbow, stroking it. "Thank you for catching me. I'd be sprawled over that grass there, laughing too hard to get back up, and there's a good chance I would have spent the night there."

Oliver shook his head. "I would never have allowed it. I would have gotten you back to the hotel, one way or another."

Hazel gasped. "Would you have carried me on your back? A real, live piggyback ride like they do in all the K-dramas?"

Oliver's face was the picture of confusion. "I...have no idea what that sentence meant. Sorry."

"In addition to be a hopeless romantic who reads way too many romance novels, I also watch way too many K-dramas. That's Korean dramas, by the way, which are seriously elite in their ability to convey *all* the feels of a good love story."

Oliver nodded. "I can't say I've seen one, but I'm tracking you so far."

"Right. It's just that in most of my favorite K-dramas, there's a scene where the female main character drinks too much and then the male main character has to carry her home on his back. You know, in a piggyback ride."

"I see. I can't say I've given—or received, for that matter—a piggyback ride since I was a small child." He looked at her askance. "In this scenario, am *I* the male main character in the K-drama you're writing in your head? What happened to your dream guy Daniel?"

"Well, duh." She glared at him. "He's not here. You are."

"I am." He squeezed her elbow gently before moving his hand back into his pocket. "And I'm not going anywhere."

Eight

The following day, Hazel and Daniel had slept in, waking up naturally after ten solid hours of rest, ready to face the new day and to do a bit of exploring. The Schuler Group had only scheduled an optional dinner for the guests that evening, with many of them still arriving that day, and so Daniel had suggested the two of them could take a bus to Termessos, one of the nearby ruins, to do some hiking.

Hazel bit her lip. "You're sure you don't want to just go walk around downtown? A hike seems a little intense for our first full day in Turkey."

"Yeah, but we don't have many days that are totally free like this, Haze. Look, I would go by myself, but it seems like it's going to be really cool, and I know you won't want to miss out on that. Come on, just join me for this one, and I promise if I want to do any more hiking and you really don't want to, I won't try to talk you into it."

"I mean, I guess..." She looked out the window, where the sun was shining in a way it rarely did back home in December. "Should we ask Oliver if he wants to join us?"

Daniel winced. "Let's meet up with him for the dinner. I'm not trying to be rude or anything, but it would be really nice if we didn't have to babysit him today."

"It's not babysitting, Daniel." She shook her head. "It's literally just friends hanging out, and I'm sure he's interested in seeing some ruins, too."

"Right, well." Daniel wasn't quite meeting her gaze. "I think he said something last night about catching up on a bit of work today. I'm sure he doesn't have the time to spare for a full day out and about like this."

"Oh, yeah?" She crossed her arms and studied her old friend. "And when exactly were the two of you alone and chatting without me? When could he possibly have told you that?"

"I don't know where you were." Daniel widened his eyes, not breaking her gaze. "Maybe you went to the bathroom, or maybe you just zoned out for a minute or something. The more I think about it, though...yeah. I'm pretty sure he told me exactly that." He smiled then. "Don't worry, I'm sure he will be done in time for dinner and the three of us can all sit together at the company dinner. Maybe you can even meet some of our other coworkers. How does that sound?"

She forced a smile. As happy as she was to be spending time with her best friend, it was tainted by the assurance she felt that he was bending the truth to get what he wanted. "That sounds good."

"Good." He nodded towards her still packed suitcase. She had kept herself out of the room for so long the day before and been so tired when she returned in the evening that she still hadn't taken more than the necessary items out of her bag. "Why don't you get ready for the day, then? Make sure you wear some appropriate shoes for hiking so I don't end up having to carry you after you twist your ankle."

That got a smile out of her as she remembered teasing Oliver about piggyback rides the night before. She raised a hand to salute. "Aye, sir. Will do."

By the time they had finished breakfast in the hotel restaurant, Daniel, who had spent the entire meal glued to his phone, had figured out their plan of attack for the day.

"Right," he said as Hazel took her last sips of coffee. "So, we should be able to take a bus pretty close to Termessos. We should pack a bag with water, maybe a snack, and some sunblock." He leaned back in his chair, his hands coming up to his neck as he stretched his elbows out to the side. "God, how good does it feel to need sunblock in December? Are you ready for this, Haze?"

Hazel nodded, noticing that since Oliver had called him out on his nickname for her, he hadn't called her "Craze" once. The nickname had never bothered her—or perhaps she had simply never let it bother her—but it did feel good to hear her name on Daniel's lips. It brought them closer together, somehow, while she could see now that "Craze" had created some sort of distance or hierarchy between them.

"I'm ready. It's going to be fun." She smiled at him, then her eyes trailed over his shoulder, where she caught a glimpse of Oliver taking a seat at a small table near the window. As if he felt her gaze on him, he looked up and directly into her eyes, the corners of his lips lifting as his hand did the same.

She returned the gesture, pulled out of their shared moment only when Daniel wheeled to look over his shoulder, his head blocking her view.

"This guy again," he mumbled. "He's everywhere, I swear." He lifted a hand towards Oliver as well, nodding a brief greeting before turning back to Hazel. "You're done? Good, then let's get moving."

Even if it didn't feel quite right to leave Oliver to his own company, Hazel followed Daniel out of the restaurant, reminding herself that a very recent past version of herself would have killed to have Daniel to herself for the day. She didn't need to feel some kind of misplaced loyalty to Oliver just because she had spent some time with him the day before and had shared her feelings with him at a level that she had been able to with few others.

When she had talked to Jack and Claire on a video call the night before, they had wanted all the details of her first day in Turkey. And she hadn't missed the looks the two of them had exchanged when she told them about her adventure with Oliver. It was obvious that both Jack and Claire were flashing back on their own meet cute in the Munich airport a year prior, that they were substituting Hazel and Oliver as the main characters in this year's holiday romance.

But they were wrong. That wasn't what had happened. If any romance were going to happen this year, it would be between Hazel and Daniel, the quintessential friends to lovers story, finally come to life. But even as she thought that, something pinched in her lower belly. Maybe Oliver had gotten into her head because it was harder this morning to see Daniel as the leading man she had assumed him to be. How was it possible that a man who could tease her like one of the guys could undergo such a change of heart that he would ever be gazing into her eyes, whispering sweet words...and that either of them would be able to take those words even remotely seriously?

That wasn't what she needed to figure out right now. What she needed to do, she reminded herself, was get ready for the day and on her way to an adventure. That was it, plain and simple. There were no complicated matters of the heart to unravel before she had even brushed her teeth and grabbed her jacket. Besides, if she was having anything remotely resembling doubts about her future with Daniel, they would pass. If there was one constant of the past decade of her life, it was the assurance that the two of them were meant to be. That wasn't the kind of thing you got over in a day, no matter how much jet-lag-induced fun you had.

Hazel hadn't expected the hike to Termessos to be such a...well...hike. When Daniel had reminded her to wear the appropriate shoes, she had imagined the place they were traveling to must have been easily accessible to the people who lived there centuries ago and that, consequently, she should be fine with her regular gym shoes.

And she had been fine with the gym shoes. It wasn't that she had needed climbing gear or hiking poles...more just the fact that there had been a *lot* of walking and that plenty of it had been at some fairly steep inclines. By the time they reached the amphitheater, she was at least as awed by the view as she was by the effort that it had taken to get there.

"It's incredible, isn't it?" Daniel's words were hushed, as if he sensed like she did that they were standing on hallowed ground.

Hazel just nodded, pausing to enjoy the view for a moment before taking out her phone to snap a few pictures. How could a camera capture the mountains and the ruins in the same shot without all of it losing its magnificence? Still, she wanted the memory of the moment, wanted something to show to her family when she got back home.

Something to show to Oliver, too, she thought, a pang as she wished for just a moment that he had joined them that day. Maybe he would take a trip here on his own before their vacation was over. Or maybe she would come back with him, if a day came that Daniel opted to do something she really didn't care to join.

"Should we keep hiking up?" Daniel asked, gesturing towards the remaining peak.

Hazel just shook her head. "This"—she gestured to the view—"is plenty for me. If you want to keep going, I'll just sit here in the amphitheater and take it all in."

Daniel nodded, taking her words in. "You could do that, I guess. I think you might get bored, though, and then you're liable to seek revenge on me for my bad behavior last night by either wandering off and making me look for you or giving me attitude for the rest of the day."

"When have I ever done either of those things?" She put her hands on her hips as she turned to face him. "I'm not a child, and I'm not going to go get lost at the mall so that you'll come look for me. And unlike someone I know, I don't give people attitude just because I'm tired or bored or hungry. Some of us have learned some basic skills to regulate our own emotions."

He held up his hands, an appeasing gesture. "It was a joke, Craze. Apparently one that hit a little too on the nose. Let's stick together, though, okay? I've watched enough horror movies to know that separating in a strange location is not the move. I wouldn't know how to explain to your brother that you slipped into an alternate dimension and got stuck there or tell your mom that apparently Jurassic Park is real, but it's in Turkey and the dinosaurs are cosplaying as ancient Greeks."

Hazel laughed and something loosened in her chest. It was nice to laugh with Daniel, not to be at these weird antagonistic odds that had been coming up more and more lately. "Fair enough. You don't mind not going all the way to the end of the hike? Heading back with me? I don't want to cut your fun short."

"It's okay. I came here to have fun with you, my bud, and that's what we've been doing. Plus, this isn't going to be my last hiking or ruin exploring day. I'm sure I'll see all I want to see and then some by the end of the trip."

"Okay, great," said Hazel, forcing her smile to stay put. If he had stopped with just the idea that the two of them spending time together was all that really mattered, her buoyant mood might have remained intact. But the reminder that it was only one of his priorities—and perhaps not even the most important one—did put a damper on things. "Let's just stay and take in the view a bit longer before we head back down." She took a seat on one of the higher seats in the amphitheater. "I just want to soak it all in. Try to feel what it felt like to be here. Imagine the people who lived here."

"Sounds good." Daniel gestured over his shoulder. "I'm just going to walk up and down the stairs a bit, get a few more steps in. Keep the heart rate up since most of the hike back is going to be downhill."

Hazel nodded, waiting to sigh until Daniel had moved out of earshot. It was moments like these when she wondered how she had managed to sustain her feelings for him for as long as she had. She shook off the thought and focused her attention back on her surroundings. The air was crisp and cool, especially against her skin that had grown damp from the exertion of the hike. The sun was shining, though, with just a few clouds in the sky that looked like they had been artfully placed there by a painter. She looked to her left and right, at the massive—and almost pristinely preserved—stadium seating around her. The remote location of the ancient city was likely partly to credit for its condition, with anyone who might want to destroy or repurpose it dissuaded by the climb.

Still, she wondered how those ancient people who had lived here had gotten water and food, how they had moved the stones enough to create the structures that were still standing. She resigned herself to searching for a book or two—or at least doing a bit of online research—to gain a basic understanding of the history of the area. When she returned home and shared photos of her trip with her family, this part in particular was bound to stir up some questions, and it wouldn't do to tell them that she didn't actually know any of the answers. Plus, it might make an interesting lesson for her students when the school year resumed.

The thought of the impending school year brought a smile to Hazel's face. Many of her colleagues, especially those who had been in the trenches of the public education system for decades longer than she had, were inclined to refer to their shared vocation as more of a hassle and pain than anything resembling a joy. And maybe it was just because she was still in those early honeymoon stages with the job—she had celebrated her fifth teaching anniversary at the end of the previous school year—but she just didn't see it that way. Oh, it wasn't that every day she was full of inspiration and hope for the future of the country and world because of the young minds she was touching. But no one made her laugh more than her students did, and nothing could boost her mood quite as much as seeing the dawn of understanding after a particularly challenging lesson.

She snapped a few more photos before tucking her phone away in her pocket, eager to get moving back towards the beginning of the trail. There was something about thinking about her classroom, about the parts of teaching that lit her up the most, that just made her itch to share it all with someone who would listen. Daniel had been there with her through the thick and thin of it—their own experience in the school system, as well as all the stress of her university and certification exams—and it wasn't so much that he wouldn't listen to her share but that she had told him all of it already.

Sure, she knew as well as anyone that sometimes you just wanted to think through your thoughts out loud, that you wanted someone there with you because it helped pull those thoughts out from wherever they might have gotten stuck in your mind. But wasn't it unfair to expect someone—even someone who loved you as much as a best friend did—to listen to you talk about the things that you did every day, like planning lessons for your classroom?

Still, Hazel was warmed by the thought that, for a little while, at least, Oliver might be willing to indulge her, to let her share what was on her mind and in her heart. And so, like a trail horse picking up its pace once the barn came into sight, she was itching to get back to the hotel.

Nine

Perhaps Daniel was more perceptive than she gave him credit for, or maybe he really was enjoying stopping to look at every plant on the side of the path. Either way, the hike back down from Termessos took at least as long as the hike up had, a fact that should have been an impossibility given its downhill nature. But if Daniel was sensing that there was someone else she was eager to spend time with...

No, Hazel wouldn't let herself believe that. Certainly, there had been a bit of weirdness between the two men at dinner the night before, but there were any number of reasons for the two of them to feel like the other was stepping on their toes. It wasn't as if Daniel could really feel jealous of Oliver for the time she was spending with him.

And if he did feel jealous...

Hazel let herself entertain the idea for just a moment before shaking it off. As much as her near-constant exposure to love stories in any and every form—on the flight to Turkey, for example, she had watched a rom com, finished listening to the audiobook of a contemporary romance, and started reading a romantic suspense—might make her expect to see real-life tropes around her at any moment, even she knew better than to expect that of Daniel. If he hadn't yet realized his love for her, it probably wasn't going to be jealousy of another man that made it all click into place.

At least, she certainly hoped that was the case. When Daniel finally realized that he loved her, she wanted it to be for something a little sweeter...maybe a new dress that really made her eyes sparkle or seeing her in a new light after she did something really kind for a little old lady.

That's, like, one step better than me taking off my glasses and him suddenly realizing I'm beautiful, she told herself, cringing at her least favorite trope. As much as she loved a good makeover story, child of the 90s that she was, she knew it wasn't the basis of any kind of lasting romance.

"Almost there," said Daniel, pulling her from her reverie as the parking lot came into view. He flashed her a grin. "It was great, wasn't it? I'm going to keep this hike as a baseline, see if I can find something similarly challenging for the upcoming days. Have you checked out the hotel gym yet, by the way?"

"You *know* I haven't." She leveled a glare at him that made him hold up his hands in surrender. "I didn't come all the way to Turkey to pick up a habit that I can't be bothered to do back home. I'm perfectly happy with yoga in my living room once a week, thank you very much."

"It's your life, Craze. Definitely not telling you how to live it." He led her over to the bus stop where they had first arrived, and they took their seats to wait for their ride back to the city.

"I think I'm going to try to meet up with Oliver when we get back to the hotel," she blurted. "Do you have any interest in hanging out?"

Daniel shook his head, his lips turned down at the corners. "Nah, I think it'll be the gym for me. What are you guys going to do? Did you make plans?"

Hazel shook her head. "No, but I figured it would be nice to check in. I got the feeling when I hung out with him yesterday that he'll be around and up for hanging out. That he might even need a friend."

"Huh." Daniel was looking out into the middle distance, willing a bus to materialize there. "It does seem weird that he didn't bring anyone with him. He seems nice enough, but maybe there's something wrong with him if no one was up for sharing a hotel room with him for two weeks." He leaned heavily against her shoulder, his laugh forced. "You'll have to report back to me and let me know if that's the case. And if you need help getting him to leave you alone, then I'll be there for you."

She barely stopped herself from rolling her eyes. "Considering I am *literally* the one who is reaching out to him, I have a feeling that is not going to be a concern." She remembered the way Oliver had reacted yesterday when they had talked about his plus one for the trip falling through, and she opted not to share it with Daniel. If he was so dead set on judging Oliver when he seemed to barely know him, she wasn't going to give him any inside scoop about her new friend.

Daniel held up a hand to assuage her. "I'm just saying. Don't you go trading me in for a newer model, Craze. You've already got a number one dude in your life, and you don't need another one."

She whirled on him then. "Do I, really? Because it seems to me that you and I might have very different ideas about what, exactly, a number one dude is." She crossed her arms over her chest. "As you might recall—it shouldn't be hard to do, since it was pretty recent—I've shared some feelings with you that you didn't exactly reciprocate. And that's fine. I'm not asking you to change the way you feel about me. But to have the audacity to tease me about being friends with another guy and to go so far as to tell me not to get a new number one dude?" She huffed out a humorless laugh. "My God, Daniel, it's like you *want* me to pine after you for my entire life rather than…I don't know…finding someone I could actually be happy with. And that really sucks."

They were both quiet for a moment, the air charged between them. Finally, Daniel broke the silence. "I didn't mean it like that, Hazel. I hope you know I really, really didn't. I would never tell you not to get involved with someone." He let out a nervous chuckle. "I never told you to have those feelings for me."

"I know you didn't," she spat. "And trust me, if I could just turn them off, then I would have by now. It's not exactly a fun thing to carry around, unreciprocated feelings."

"I don't know what to say. I'm sorry." He tentatively rested a finger on her forearm, waiting until she deigned to look at him again before he removed it. "I'll be happy for you when you meet someone. I'll sit in the front row at your wedding—or better yet, I'll be your bridesman, if you'll let me." He pulled a face. "Just don't tell me that guy is going to be Oliver, okay?"

Hazel sighed. "I don't know what you're so opposed to about him. He's a really good guy, Daniel." She forced her loose hair behind her ear. "But no, in the few hours we've spent together, there has been no discussion of marriage, so I think you're safe on that front." She was hollow, scooped out from the inside like a pumpkin turning into a Halloween decoration. "You're probably safe from having to watch me get married to anyone, honestly. I can't even imagine it."

"Hey." Daniel leaned against her shoulder, then leaned away and came back again with more force, trying to jolt her out of her doldrums. "I know I'm not the expert on relationships and that I don't really know anything about unrequited love—"

"Oh rub it in, why don't you," she cried, a watery quality in her voice that hadn't been there before. "Why don't you just say, 'Everyone I like always likes me back' while you're at it."

"I mean..."

She wanted to wipe that shit-eating grin off his face.

"No, hear me out," he said. "I may not be an expert on any of this—and you should definitely talk to Claire if you're looking for one of those—but I know you're going to find it some day. The real deal, Haze. Someone who will see you in all the ways that you are special and amazing and the best and who will want to hold on to you for all of those reasons."

"And it's not going to be you." The words hurt coming out, surprising her even as she spoke them.

He shook his head, a kindness in his eyes that answered the sadness in hers. It wasn't new information, wasn't anything she hadn't heard before, hadn't tormented herself into replaying in her mind after every failed love confession.

But that didn't mean it didn't hurt to have it confirmed. That it didn't cause a stinging in the back of her eyes that made her want to retreat to a blanket fort and not reemerge until Daniel was long gone.

Hazel forced a smile and blinked rapidly to clear her eyes. "Well, as long as you're sure there will be someone," she said, only briefly letting her gaze meet Daniel's.

He just nodded. "You're going to be just fine, Hazel. Better than fine. You'll have to wait and see, but in the meantime, you can trust me."

She was quiet as she took in his words. When the bus arrived and they made their way into the seats, she sat next to the window and took in the views of the city and coast as they returned to the hotel. She should, as she gazed at the turquoise water, be thinking about how to move forward, how to get back to equilibrium after her unexpected outburst with Daniel. Staring out the window on long car rides had always been some of her best thinking time as a child, always the time when she was the most likely to have a great idea or some random inspiration.

But it wasn't like that today. Today, as she stared out the window, she only felt numb. She was numb and tired and she just wanted to be somewhere dark and cozy and, most importantly, alone. Or at least not with Daniel.

As if he were reading her thoughts, Daniel cleared his throat to get her attention. She turned her head slightly to take him in, and he gave her a hesitant smile.

"I was thinking," he began. "It might be nice for just you and Oliver to go to dinner tonight." He let out a self-deprecating chuckle. "I'm guessing you're sick of me by now, and you both might have a better time if I'm not there, making it all awkward and weird. What do you say, Haze? How does that sound?"

She turned back to the window, murmuring her assent. She didn't know how good the company she gave Oliver would be, but if she didn't have to sit next to Daniel and pretend everything was okay, then that was already a win.

Back at the hotel, Daniel made a beeline for the gym, taking a change of clothes and his laptop bag with him. "I'll just stay out of your hair for the rest of the day," he said, his smile holding a forced casualness. "Tomorrow is a new day."

"Indeed." She nodded once, then let herself into the room, where she collapsed face-first onto her bed with a groan. Her earlier plans to check in with Oliver, to go do some exploring before they all met up for dinner, had dissipated with whatever little hope had accrued in her heart since her last spurned love confession to Daniel. She wondered, for a moment, if she should see a professional about the chronic nature of her feelings for him. This couldn't be normal, could it? Wouldn't most self-respecting women move on a little more quickly than this? And was she living out the literal definition of insanity, repeating the same thing over again and expecting different results?

All she could manage was to dig her phone out of her pocket and fire off a quick message to Oliver.

"Meet at 7 for dinner. Just you and me tonight."

She didn't expect any response from him, just shoved her phone under her pillow as she wiggled her shoes off her feet, slowly working her way under the blankets. From the fluffy recesses, a vibration sounded, and she retrieved her phone to find a new message from Oliver.

"It's a date, then. Already looking forward to it."

Hazel groaned again. He was too nice, and he was humoring her. That much was clear. It was like receiving a compliment from her brother or her mom telling her she was a real catch. Sure, it might give her a little boost, but she knew its sincerity paled in comparison to its intention to uplift her spirits.

There was another vibration then, another message.

"You okay? Need me to come find you?"

She fumbled to respond. The last thing she needed was Oliver descending in all his glory to find her wallowing. No, he could have the pleasure of her company at dinner and not a moment sooner. She was going to take every second available for her wallowing in the meantime. She pulled herself out for just a moment to respond before letting herself tumble back down into the depths of her mind.

"All good. See you then."

· ❤ · ❤ · ❤ · ❤ · ❤ ·

Hazel's best laid plans had been foiled, as her sadness and heaviness were replaced by something new, a curiosity and anticipation that felt foreign. An hour before she was due to meet Oliver, she straightened up against her headboard and sighed. She couldn't stay lying down one moment longer, and she was keenly aware that she was about to meet a handsome man—*a friend*, she reminded herself, *only a friend*—for dinner with no buffer at all.

"No chaperone," she told herself out loud, before chuckling at the words. Still, though. Even if Oliver was just a friend, wouldn't it be nice to put in a little effort, to show up looking her best and hope that the effort she put in on the outside would have an effect on her inside, as well?

She hauled herself to her feet and towards her suitcase, where she fished out another dress, a bag with the jewelry she hadn't bothered to look through the day before, a curling iron, and her full makeup bag. If he had seen the "slight effort applied" Hazel preview the day before, he was going to get the full show today. She selected an off-the-shoulder number, a deep navy that always got her just the right kind of compliments—they were of the "oh you look stunning" variety, *not* of the "oh, that dress is gorgeous, where did you get it?" variety, and that difference was crucially important.

After showering, taming her hair into some messy waves with the curling iron, pumping her makeup up a notch with a bright red lip and a little extra effort put into her eyeliner, she was ready. As she looked in the mirror, she couldn't help but notice that she *did* feel better. The woman staring back at her was a better match for who she knew herself to be on the inside than the one with tear-streaked cheeks and a vacant stare who had looked into that same mirror an hour before had been.

It didn't matter that this evening was, at best, a rehearsal for the kind of date she might go on in the future. It mattered that, when given the opportunity to take the easy exit and spend the evening wearing her sweatpants and watching the hotel TV, she had put in the effort she knew she deserved.

"I know self care isn't all face masks and beauty treatments," she told her reflection with a quirked eyebrow, "but I can't help it if dragging myself into the shower and playing with my makeup afterwards makes me feel more like the human version of myself than the swamp thing that plays her in a movie." She nodded at herself, slipping her purse over her shoulder. "Alright then. Here goes nothing."

Ten

Oliver was waiting right where she had expected him to be, his back facing her as he took in the view directly in front of the hotel. The sun had set, but there was still enough of the sea visible that she knew his eyes, like hers, couldn't help but be drawn to it.

As she approached him, he turned, as if he knew the footsteps he was hearing on the hotel's marble floor couldn't belong to anyone but her. She took him in, dressed in a button-down shirt, a pair of pants that fit him like he actually knew how to dress himself, and leather shoes. But what stuck out the most were his eyes. They had fixed on hers, and they hadn't drifted away, apart from taking the quickest stroll down her body to take in her full outfit.

"Hi," he greeted her, pulling her in for a quick kiss on the cheek. "You look beautiful, as always."

Hazel pulled a face. "Oh, come on. I put in way too much effort this evening for you to pretend I look this good on a normal day." She did a quick, self-conscious spin. "Please. Admire my handiwork. This hair. This makeup. This whole outfit, to be honest."

"I am admiring all of it," said Oliver, and she could see from the path his eyes took that he was doing just that. "And while I agree that the dress is something special, I stand by my earlier statement. You are as beautiful as always."

"Oh. Okay then." She felt herself deflate slightly, but she forced a smile as she gave him a pointed once-over. "You look very handsome yourself."

"Hazel." Her eyes met his, and there was something unfamiliar there. "I'm not saying you always look beautiful to downplay the effort you apparently put into this evening. I'm...well, I guess I'm just forcing you to confront the possibility that some of us find you beautiful only in a sexy dress and some of us would find you beautiful in sweatpants." He gave her a sheepish smile. "And we might be clueless enough about women's fashion and style to not be able to tell much of a difference between them." He offered her his arm, and she tucked her hand into the crook of his elbow. "Just know that I am honored to have you on my arm, and I'm sure I'm going to be the envy of everyone who sees us."

"Good," she said with a humorless laugh as they stepped out of the hotel. "Frankly, I could use the ego boost."

Oliver looked down at her with concern in his eyes. "What happened today? I was worried about you, but I wanted to respect your space, too. I would have showed up at the door of your hotel if I'd thought the gesture would have been remotely welcome."

Hazel pulled a face. "Sorry about that. But that's sort of what I was afraid of, and I just wanted to be alone."

"No, nothing to be sorry about," he said, directing her towards the sidewalk where they began walking in the same direction as the restaurant they had visited the previous evening. "I'm glad you took care of yourself rather than trying to please someone else." He paused, clearing his throat. "Did something happen with Daniel? Where is he tonight?"

"Oh, it sure did. And it…" Hazel stopped in her tracks, taking in Oliver and the scenery behind him before shaking her head. "You know what? No. I already let that particular conversation ruin one of the few afternoons I get to spend here in Turkey. I could have been exploring the old city or searching for sea glass this afternoon, but instead I spent that time hiding under my blankets, moping around about the same guy that I do the same thing about back in New York. I already let it ruin my afternoon, and I don't want to let it ruin my evening." She fixed her gaze on Oliver's then, darting from one iris to the other. "Is that okay with you? Can we leave Daniel behind for the evening, find something else to talk about?"

He put his hand over hers for just a second, giving it a squeeze. "Absolutely. It's just you and me tonight. We can do whatever you want, and we can *definitely* talk about whatever you want." He tipped his head back towards the sidewalk, asking the question with his eyes if they could keep on going.

Hazel nodded, continuing on with a new pep in her step. "Where are we going, by the way? The same place as last night? Because there are definitely a few more things on that menu I'd like to try. And a few things I'd order again just because they were so good the first time around. That salad…" She trailed off, the focus of her eyes going hazy as she remembered the pesto salad dressing the restaurant had used.

"It was amazing," Oliver agreed. "And I'm happy to confirm you liked it so much. I'll take you back there again before our time here is over."

There was a flutter of excitement in Hazel's belly at his words. This wasn't a one-off thing between them. He wasn't entertaining her simply because Daniel wasn't available. He was making plans for their future.

Hold on a second there, girlie, she thought. *Planning to eat another meal with you isn't exactly the same thing as planning to move in together.*

Hazel would have shaken her head at the absurdity of her inner monologue, if she hadn't been accompanied by someone who was bound to ask her why she was twitching and what was causing it. But seriously, why had her brain even gone there? Oliver was a friend, and considering that he was a friend with whom she had shared her feelings for another man within moments of meeting, he was the furthest thing from a romantic prospect.

It was a refreshing change of pace, actually, to have a male friend without all the baggage. A friendship that was actually devoid of romantic possibility and the sort of interactions that made her want to stay up into the wee hours of the night, documenting every interaction in her journal so she could interpret and reinterpret his every comment, glance, and gesture.

In contrast, with Oliver she could just let herself have fun. They could explore and eat delicious food and laugh and talk and, all the while, she could breathe. She wasn't wondering if she was too much, if she was coming on too strong, or trying to read his mind. Everything was at the surface, from the fact that they clearly both enjoyed each other's company to all the stupid jokes, needless observations, and comfortable silences that they shared.

Oliver steered her to the left just as the fish restaurant came into view, taking them down another street she hadn't even been aware of crossing the night before. They walked a few more blocks before arriving at an elegant restaurant—and a popular one, judging by the number of people milling about by the door.

Hazel turned to him with a raised eyebrow. "How do you know this place? Have you secretly been to Antalya before? Or are we gambling on the trustworthiness of a Yelp review right now?"

He rubbed the back of his neck as he peered through the window, the low lighting and romantic ambience apparent even from outside on the street. "I asked the concierge at the hotel for a recommendation, the kind of place he would take a date to." He looked into her eyes then, as if he were daring her to ask the follow-up question that must surely be on her mind.

"You, uh…er…" She almost plowed ahead, but when an emergency exit appeared, she took it. "Oh, you mean, like, to make sure you found the kind of place he thought was nice? Like if you hadn't told him to imagine it being for a date, he might have directed you to the nearest McDonald's, imagining that's what an American in his city might feel most comfortable with."

Oliver shook his head, laughing softly. "Something like that," he said. He reached for the door then, holding it open for her. "Shall we?"

The restaurant, as it turned out, specialized in grilled meats, and judging by the sampling of dishes Hazel and Oliver had tasted, they had earned every bit of their reputation as one of the best restaurants in the city. From the lamb and chicken to the meatballs and liver—*yes, even the liver had been a delicacy*, a thought that Hazel couldn't remember ever thinking in her lifetime—the simple food prepared to perfection had made it a meal she wouldn't soon forget.

Of course, the restaurant had mastered its ambiance, too, and if Hazel had been there with anyone but Oliver, she probably would have been overwhelmed or outright intimidated by its sultry and romantic vibes. The lighting was low, the booth they shared the sort that a couple could cozy right up next to each other and feed each other bites off their plates. At least, that was what she suspected was happening at their neighboring booths, though she was pointedly keeping her eyes on her own paper, a vital lesson from elementary school coming in clutch.

But between the flickering of low candlelight, the solicitous waiter, the mouthwatering starters, and the bottle of wine they opted to share, it certainly did feel like a date.

Whenever those thoughts cropped up, though, Hazel just looked at the man sitting across from her, smiled, then lobbed the most off-the-cuff remark at him she could think of, reminding them both—not that he needed it, she was sure—that they were friends and that none of this needed to be weird. Once, she had asked him with a totally straight face what his favorite kind of soup was, and once she had quipped that toilets without bidets should be illegal. Both times, he had laughed, smiled, and gone right along with her, ready to "yes, and" any joke she sent his way.

When the waiter had approached to ask about dessert, Oliver gave her a tentative glance. "We're still thinking about it," he told the waiter, asking him to come back again in a few moments.

"We don't really need it, do we?" she offered, reading his hesitation. "The meal will be expensive enough without it—and we're splitting it, so don't even try to tell me we aren't—and we definitely don't *need* more calories at this point in the day."

Oliver shook his head. "That wasn't what I was thinking at all, and I'm dismayed to learn that you are, in fact, a quitter." His eyes flashed as he leaned across the table. "What about going somewhere else for dessert? I heard there's a great baklava place, and they do a lot of unique varieties there, like a cold baklava that has chocolate on it, which...I mean...how good does that sound?" He glanced away. "I mean, assuming they're still open."

"Oh, yeah, right." Hazel leaned back, crossing her arms. "You and I both know you already checked to see if they're open. Your little concierge friend surely recommended this place, too, and you wouldn't have brought it up if you hadn't already scoped it out." An idea occurred to her then, and she narrowed her eyes at Oliver. "*Did* you already scope these places out? You walked here tonight like you knew where you were going. Did you map out the route beforehand or something?"

Oliver nodded, his expression matter of fact. "Of course. I wasn't going to spend our first date dragging you all over the neighborhood and getting lost. We already had enough of an experience with hangriness last night." He winced and held up his hands in apology. "Sorry about that. Wasn't going to bring our mutual friend up, and yet there I did it."

"It's okay." She reached a hand towards him, tapping the table. "Daniel is a fact of our lives, and we're definitely going to talk about him again. Hell, we're going to see him again soon, too." She chuckled nervously. "I'm literally sleeping in the same room as him, so if I don't see him, we've got bigger problems. Either that will mean I've lost my eyesight or else Daniel has been eaten by bears. Are there bears in Antalya?"

"I haven't seen any," said Oliver, gamely playing along. "So, to bring it back to our original topic, you aren't totally judging me for doing a practice run to get to the restaurant before our date?"

Our date. He had called it a date once before, and she had let it slide, unwilling or unable to read too much into it. But now that he had said it again, it was as if he wanted to test her, to see how she would react to it.

"Is that what this is? A date?"

If the room were better lit, maybe she would have seen Oliver's cheeks turn red, but in the candlelight, she told herself she was imagining it. "What else do you call it when two people get dressed up and eat a meal?" he asked, his gaze not quite meeting hers.

"Dinner?" she offered. "An outing, maybe. It doesn't matter, not really. I guess it's just that *date* tends to have a romantic connotation, and I'm trying really hard these days to detox myself from adding romantic undertones to my friendships with men." She offered him a bashful smile. "As you no doubt noticed, I'm a real mess in that department."

"You're not a mess, Hazel." Oliver's hand briefly landed on top of hers, where it was still placed on the table. "Even in the short time that I've known you, I can tell you that you are many things, but none of them are a mess."

"What, then? What would you call a grown woman who's still carrying around a crush like she's twelve years old, if not a mess?" She didn't look away, knowing that her words had come out as a challenge, but not caring. Anyone could say something like that—it was the nice thing to say, after all—but that didn't mean they could back it up. And she had no room for platitudes and empty compliments.

Oliver was quiet as he gathered his thoughts—*or as he, more likely, tried to come up with enough bullshit to make her ego feel assuaged*, she thought. When he spoke, his tone was steady. "I would say that that woman is—that *you* are—a deeply loyal and hopeful soul. The sort of person who can't stop caring about someone even when maybe she should, even when they might not deserve it as much as she thinks they do. The sort of person who can't bring herself to keep someone out, even when letting them in hurts her. And that doesn't make her a mess." He gave her a sad smile. "That just makes me hope that she'll learn to set boundaries before she gets hurt."

Hazel blinked rapidly. "I mean...yikes. If this really *was* a date, I think the mood would have been killed by the psychoanalysis." She forced a laugh. "You might be onto something there, though."

"I don't mean to be harsh, or to suggest that Daniel isn't deserving of your friendship. He's a good guy, and he definitely does deserve to have a good friend. I'm just not sure he should be looked at through the particular heart-shaped goggles you may have been wearing for the past years. Not when those goggles make you think he's above reproach, a perfect, immaculate being, while you walk around here on earth with the rest of us mortals, referring to yourself as a mess. If you're a mess, Hazel, then what does that make Daniel? I'd rather you see both of you as humans than put one of you on a pedestal and poke fun at the other one."

"Yeah." She swallowed. "Well, it's something to think about."

"Hey." When she looked up, his eyes were on her, and there was kindness in them. "The other thing I said, about being hopeful. That's amazing, Hazel. In a world where so many people fixate on bad news, on what's going wrong, on what's falling apart, you have the unique ability to hope for something good."

She huffed. "Hoping that my friend will fall in love with me does not make me some sort of role model."

"It's not just that. You're hoping for a better future for yourself and for him, but you're hoping for it for your students, too. I see the way you look at everyone we meet, at every new thing you encounter. You see the best. You see the possibilities. You see the potential for magic, even where the rest of us might be inclined only to see the shortcomings."

"I'm trying to imagine that this mystical creature of which you speak is me, but I'm sorry, Oliver. She sounds completely unfamiliar. Made up, actually."

"It's what I see, Hazel. I may not have known you long, but I see you."

She looked at him then, let herself *really* look at him for the first time since they had started talking about messes. "You really do, don't you?"

Oliver nodded, holding out his hand for her, and she slipped hers inside. She gave it a squeeze, then smiled.

"Then we'd better go check out that baklava, huh? It might be the best thing we've ever tasted!"

Eleven

By the time Hazel returned to her room, she was full of four different kinds of baklava and more warm and fuzzy feelings than she had known she could contain. She had let Oliver walk her to the door of her hotel room—had hoped they would not find Daniel inside—and had given him a tight hug before she slipped away inside.

"Thank you for a lovely evening," she had said before scowling up at him. "I wish you had let me split the cost of the meal with you, though."

He had held up his hands in mock protest. "It couldn't be helped," he had said. "I had already run my credit card when I made the reservation this afternoon. It was out of my hands."

"Well, the next one is going to be on me," she replied.

"Hmm," he murmured with a small nod. "We'll see. I'm writing off all my meals for the trip, so I would hate to see you pay for one of them. Plus, I like feeding you."

Her cheeks had heated at that. "We'll figure it out next time, then, I guess." She bumped her knuckles against his upper arm—against his very firm upper arm, she couldn't help noting—and then said goodnight before slipping inside her room.

Inside, she deflated in relief at finding the room empty, letting herself sag against the door as a sigh escaped her lips. The evening had surpassed her every expectation of it, and she couldn't quite process all that had happened. From the way they had both cranked their efforts up a notch with their sartorial choices to the palpable nerves, not to mention the deep eye contact and a flirty vibe she was almost sure she wasn't imagining...what had happened, exactly, that evening?

Had she really gone on a date with Oliver?

Oh sure, he had called it just that—had even clarified it, in case she had been in doubt—but the problem wasn't the word. The problem was what it meant. Did it mean the same thing to him that it did to her? Did she *want* it to mean what she was starting to feel like it meant? Did she really want to be kick-your-heels-in-the-air-and-giggle giddy about going on a date with Oliver?

It wasn't as if she felt disloyal to Daniel. It was abundantly clear for the umpteenth time that he didn't require or want that particular flavor of loyalty from her. If anything, her hesitation where Daniel was concerned probably had more to do with being a quitter, with giving up on something—*someone*—that she had wanted for so long.

Hazel sighed again. If she was being honest with herself, it wasn't really about giving up on him. The thing that was twisting her gut, that felt equal parts exciting and nausea-inducing—okay, maybe the nausea-inducing part had a clear majority advantage—was how everyone would react to the news that she had fallen for another male friend of hers.

Oh, Daniel might be slightly relieved to have the pressure taken off him. But it would probably be a long time before he could take her seriously as a human again. And what about everyone else? What about Jack and Claire? For all their insistence that Hazel should seek out her own love story, they were likely to be unimpressed that she had managed to fall for the first man who had paid her any attention.

What, for that matter, would Oliver think of it? He had befriended her under the pretense that she was a safe figure in the friend zone, someone to talk to about anything and everything, with no concern of feelings developing. Had she really managed to mess everything up this badly, and this quickly, by developing feelings for him?

Hazel groaned as she made her way into the bathroom to wash off her makeup. "What feelings?" she grumbled into the mirror. "Are there feelings? Do I have feelings for Oliver? Or do I just like attention and tonight had all the trappings of an actual date, so I just let myself get carried away with it?"

By the time she had scrubbed every last inch of mascara from her face and ruined one washcloth in the process, she had convinced herself that it was all a figment of her imagination.

"There's nothing I need to wrap my head around tonight," she told herself as she changed into her pajamas and brushed her teeth. "Anyone can get excited about a guy after a full night of playing dress up. Haven't we all had our hearts broken at a middle school dance by a boy we never even looked at twice in algebra class?" She tucked her hair up into a messy bun, giving herself one last pep talk in the mirror. "See how it all goes in the light of day. There probably isn't even anything worth getting all worked up about."

She switched off the lights and tucked herself into her bed, only wondering for a moment where Daniel was, before her head hit the pillow and she drifted off into a dreamless sleep.

Thankfully, Daniel must have remembered to set an alarm whenever he came back to the room, because Hazel was awakened bright and early to the sound of it blaring from his phone on the far nightstand.

She groaned, pulling a pillow over her head and wishing for silence for just a moment before she bolted upright, remembering the reason the alarm had been set. This time, it wasn't an early wake-up call for Daniel to get the best spot at the gym. It was the welcome breakfast that the Schuler Group had arranged, and she needed to be there, too.

The flutter of nerves that she felt at the awareness that she was about to be subjected to the scrutiny of Daniel's boss and coworkers paled in comparison to what she felt when he sat up and smiled sheepishly at her. "Morning, Haze," he said, before getting up and shuffling into the bathroom.

"Morning," she responded, just as the door closed. They really had left things awkwardly the day before, hadn't they? Where did they go from here? How were they going to get back to being the Daniel and Hazel that they'd been ever since seventh grade math class?

She had to hope that time would do its classic move and heal all wounds. For the moment, though, the least she could contribute to that particular reality was making sure he wasn't late for his company breakfast and that the plus one he had brought from home reflected well on him. She forced herself out of bed and began rooting around for the closest approximation of business casual she could find in her bag, finally settling on a pair of dark wash jeans, a sleeveless blouse, and a lightweight cardigan. Now to do something about her hair…

Daniel emerged from the bathroom, looking more awake than he had when he had entered. "Did you have a nice night?" he asked, turning his back to her as he began to dig through his own clothes.

"I did. The restaurant was really good." She gritted her teeth at the stilted nature of her speech. "How about you? What did you get up to?"

"Yeah, it was a good night. I went out with some other coworkers. We got some food, even happened upon a little nightlife."

A pang of something like fear, high in her chest. She forced a laugh to cover it. "You went out dancing? That doesn't sound like you."

"Yeah, I did. It was actually fun, and I'm just as surprised as you are."

When he glanced over at her, she made sure she was smiling. Even though she wanted to ask him if he had met someone or if one of the coworkers he had been with was someone he was interested in, she forced herself not to. They were still trying to rebuild the damage her feelings had done yesterday, and it was going to be a lot easier to do that if she could manage to stay breezy. The second she started playing the jealous girlfriend, any forward progress they had made would be set back almost as far as the first time she had confessed her feelings to him, the first real time he had rejected her.

"Well, I would love to see whatever moves you busted out on the dance floor," she said with a self consciously wide grin. "And I do hope they've improved a bit since those high school dances after the home football games."

Daniel scoffed. "Oh, you ain't seen nothing yet, Craze. Just you wait. When you see these moves, you aren't even going to know what hit you." He gave her an oblivious smile. "Hey, you know what I just realized? Maybe the next time we are at an event with dancing together, maybe it'll be a wedding. And more specifically, maybe it'll be Jack and Claire's wedding. That would be pretty sweet, wouldn't it?"

Now it was her turn to scoff. "Really? They aren't even engaged, and Claire is practically already a member of the family. I can't really imagine the two of them doing the full wedding thing, Claire in a whole gown and Jack in a tuxedo."

"I don't know," he said with a shrug. "I get that they're happy the way they are, but...well, isn't there something kind of special about celebrating your love in front of everyone you know? I'm not saying they have to do the giant wedding that you go into debt for, but at least a party with some good music to get me out on the dance floor."

"Maybe." The more she thought about a wedding like that, the more she realized it held no appeal for her. It wasn't about her brother or Claire, though she did consider herself and Jack close enough that Daniel's insinuation that he might know her own brother's wishes better than her made her feel *deeply* prickly.

The point, though, was that if she were the one staring down the barrel of an impending marriage, she wouldn't be thinking about the big wedding, the event hall, or the hundreds of guests with anything but anxiety. Given the option to take her nearest and dearest away for a vacation instead—she couldn't help but think somewhere like Antalya would be perfect for that—and just slip a wedding ceremony into one of the evenings there, she would choose that every time.

"I'll make sure to let Jack know you're really gunning for the big wedding. Any other wishes I should pass on to him?" And then, fueled by a courage she wouldn't take an extra moment to analyze, she asked her question. "Is that what you would want? A big wedding like that?" She laughed, forcing lightness into what felt deathly serious. "An opportunity to show off your killer moves?"

"Oh, definitely," said Daniel. "You know that, Craze. You know how I love a good wedding."

"Hmm." She nodded and gave him a tight-lipped smile. How many weddings of their mutual friends had they attended? How many times had those evenings ended with variations on a heartsick Hazel confiding to her mom, her journal, or one of her few friends who would still listen, that she just didn't know why that couldn't be her and Daniel? Or why he always had to dance with the prettiest bridesmaids, dragging her out on the dance floor only for the Funky Chicken or the Electric Slide. Add in a few glasses of wine, and there might even be tears.

"Well, I truly hope that your dreams of being a prince for a day come true," she said, straightening up with her clothes in her arms. "You mind if I take the bathroom?"

When they entered the hotel's restaurant, it had been transformed. There was a sign at the door that announced in English and Turkish that it was closed for a private event, that guests who weren't affiliated with the Schuler Group were invited to take their breakfasts to go or to enjoy complimentary room service.

Just outside the restaurant, an elderly man wearing suspenders and a giant smile was waiting, two small children ducking behind him. He was greeting each guest in turn, and Hazel felt herself relaxing as they moved towards him, his energy that of a grandfather or a sage elder from a children's movie.

"Daniel!" the man cried, reaching out for a handshake and then pulling him in for a hug that seemed to surprise in its strength, judging by the way Daniel stumbled. "Charlie, Minnie, come out from there and say hi to Mr. Martin. This is one of my best guys!"

The children stepped tentatively outside, smiling and nodding and shaking Daniel's hand.

"These are my grandchildren, Charlie and Minnie," said the man, nodding towards a table. "Their mother is just over there with my wife. I tried to get the whole family to join me here for a welcome line, but they were pretty insistent that this was neither a wedding nor a funeral and that they therefore would not be doing that." His eyes landed on Hazel just then and she saw a spark of recognition and delight here. "And who is this?" His eyes darted to Daniel and then back to Hazel in quick suggestion. "Your girlfriend, I believe? If I'm remembering correctly, you aren't married yet. Hurry up and introduce me, Daniel."

"Mr. Schuler, this is Hazel, my best friend," said Daniel, gesturing towards Hazel. "And Hazel, this is Mr. Schuler. He's the founder and CEO of the Schuler Group and, coincidentally, the best boss any of us have ever had."

"It's really nice to meet you, Mr. Schuler," said Hazel, stepping forward to accept the older man's hand, surprising her with both its grip and its warmth. "I've heard only good things about you from Daniel."

"Oh, that." Mr. Schuler waved a dismissive hand. "I suppose it's nice that he says things like that, but that isn't what we're here to talk about today, is it? We all earned a vacation, and damn it, we're going to enjoy it! Now why don't you two go find your seats..." He turned to take in the room, his eyes landing somewhere in the middle distance. "Oh! I see Oliver waving to you, and it looks like there are some empty seats at his table." He patted Daniel on the back, pushing him in the direction of Oliver's table as he winked at Hazel. "I'll see you two later. Enjoy your breakfast."

Hazel hurried to fall into step next to Daniel. "Well, he is *adorable*. I don't know why you never told me that."

He shot her a glance. "Believe it or not, I tend not to think about my workplace superiors in terms of their adorability." After a beat, he dropped his voice and leaned towards her. "He definitely is a pretty precious human, though. I think he's the whole reason middle management exists, because Mr. Schuler is just too nice and pure and good for this world. Nobody would ever get any constructive criticism if it were left to him, but they would all walk away with a piece of candy."

"Love that about him. I have a feeling we would be great friends."

They had arrived at Oliver's table then, and he got to his feet to shake Daniel's hand and give Hazel a kiss on the cheek. She felt herself blushing, struggling to lift her gaze to his eyes, and she worried for the first time that the feelings she had dismissed as inconvenient manipulations of date-like circumstances might actually survive in the light of day...

But then Mr. Schuler was tapping on a microphone and clearing his throat and Hazel and Daniel were being ushered into the two empty seats. Without meaning to, Hazel found herself sitting next to Oliver, her chair closer to his than to Daniel's and, much to her surprise, she also found herself leaving the chair right where it was, close enough to Oliver to feel the heat of his skin, the gravitational force of his gaze.

Oh, I'm in trouble, she thought, turning away from both to face the entrance, and Mr. Schuler.

Twelve

"Welcome, Schuler Group employees and loved ones," said Mr. Schuler with that smile Hazel had already come to recognize as his trademark. "It is my sincere joy to welcome you to our workplace retreat here in Turkey." He shook his head, as if he couldn't quite believe it.

"When my dear darling wife Glenda suggested we take the whole workplace abroad to celebrate both the company's anniversary and a record year, I'll admit I looked at her like she had grown a second head." He paused for the laughter that trickled through the room. "But, if I've learned anything after sixty years with Glenda, it's that she's right about most everything. And also, I shouldn't look at her like she's grown a second head unless I like finding myself in the doghouse. And I most certainly do not like finding myself in the doghouse." He gave his wife a cheeky smile.

"Glenda and I have always loved traveling. When we were newlyweds, as soon as we could afford it, we got our passports and started planning our first international trip.

For the first few years, heading across the border to Canada was all we could swing, but you'd better believe we made the most of it. And then, just when we had started to think it wasn't going to happen for us, we learned we were about to become parents to our sweet Nora, and I think we all know what having a newborn does to travel. Why, of course, it makes it much easier and much more pleasant for everyone involved." His eyes were squinting with his laughter as he mouthed, "I love you," to his daughter, who was hanging her head. "Glenda and I took a babymoon cruise around the Mediterranean, and we fell in love with this part of the world. We've taken every opportunity we could to come back for a visit, and there wasn't even a second option when we started thinking about where to take the company."

He paused, waiting for any chatter to die down and the attention in the room to be fully directed his way. "We really hope this is a magical time for you. Now, in keeping with being able to write off the full expenses of this little retreat of ours as a work expense, we're going to have to have a couple of 'meetings.'" He raised his wrinkled fingers to make air quotes around the word. "But I promise that while we show you the annual profit-and-loss report, there will at least be cocktails and appetizers. We have a lot to celebrate, and we wanted to do it with all of you. Oh, I know I could have given myself a million dollar bonus"—there was that giant grin again—"but what am I going to do with that money at this point in my life?" He gestured around the room. "This is what I want. I won't go as far as to say that we're all family—my daughter has informed me that is the kind of thing bosses say in order to extort unpaid labor—so I'll just tell you that I love you all and I'm glad you're here. Now, let's eat!"

As he left his position at the front of the room and took his seat with his family, Hazel turned back around to face the rest of the table. It was a round table, and the only two familiar people at it were Daniel and Oliver. Across the table from them, there were two couples, one of which had, by her best estimation, a 7-year-old girl sitting with them. The girl made eye contact with Hazel, smiling shyly at her before turning to tug on her mom's sleeve.

Hazel was still smiling back when she realized Oliver was leaning towards her. She jolted back in surprise at his nearness, flushing with embarrassment as the others at the table turned their attention to her. "Sorry," she said. "Don't mind me."

She turned back to Oliver then, hissing, "Don't surprise me like that. I'm not trying to get a reputation with Daniel's coworkers as the jumpy, weird girl."

"Sorry," he said, a smile in his voice. "I didn't realize that me wanting to speak with you and ask you how you slept could be so shocking. I will never do it again."

"See that you don't." There was something about his earnest nature, the sincerity of his apology despite it being for something so silly, that melted whatever icy exterior she had tried to put in place. "And I slept really well, actually, thanks for asking. How about you?"

"I tossed and turned a bit. A lot on my mind, I guess." His gaze was intent on her, the eye contact breaking only when he reached for his napkin, arranging his silverware beside his plate as if it were his most pressing need, despite the breakfast servers not even arriving at their table yet.

"Oh?" Hazel asked, hoping for a bit more to work with. "I'm happy to be a listening ear if you've got something on your mind. Goodness knows you've provided me that service already, and it would be nice to repay your kindness."

Oliver nodded. "I'm not sure that will be necessary." He darted a quick, reassuring smile in her direction. "It seems, perhaps, that if there's nothing keeping you up at nights, then there shouldn't be anything keeping me up, either."

Well, that was cryptic. She frowned, and she was this close to escorting Oliver bodily from the room, steering him by his elbow if need be, when Daniel popped a hand on her shoulder.

"Craze, come meet my coworkers." As she leaned back towards him, Daniel gestured across the table. "This is Austin and that's Elliot. Austin and Elliot, this is my friend."

"It's really nice to meet you both," said Hazel, standing up to shake their hands across the table, doing the same with the partners and child that were sitting there as well.

"Sorry, I didn't catch your name," said Austin with an apologetic smile. "Was it...*Craze*? That can't be right."

"It's Hazel," Oliver spoke up, shooting an icy glance at Daniel, who seemed to be laughing behind the hand he had raised to his mouth. "Hazel Holloway."

"Ah, Hazel," said Austin with a nod, brow furrowing at Oliver. "Are you two friends as well?"

"We are," said Oliver with the sort of confidence Hazel could only admire. The way he spoke two words with a surety where she would have offered at least twenty full of parentheticals was something that should be studied.

Still, she couldn't help herself from offering a bit more explanation. "We just met a few days ago," she said. "But we're fast friends. Plus, it helps keep me out of Daniel's hair, so that's a win for everyone."

"What do you do, Hazel?" asked Elliot, taking a sip of coffee.

The reality of sustained attention from a group of strangers meant that Hazel's cheeks were full of at least fifty percent of the blood in her body, and that amount was unlikely to decrease until they had all shifted their attention somewhere else. She gritted her teeth, swallowed, and smiled across the table. "I'm a teacher," she said "I teach third grade at a public school in New York. It's just what I always wanted to do, actually. Sort of a dream come true, you could say."

When she found herself rambling, she darted a glance in Daniel's direction. This would be a great time for a best friend to swoop in and do a bit of rescuing. Diverting the attention from her would be a welcome strategy, as would offering a bit of extra detail, anything to legitimize her statements.

Instead, she saw her friend with his eyes fixed down on the table, where he was reading something on his phone. Just as she was about to change the subject, to sink so low as to ask the others where they lived and what the weather was like there, Oliver spoke up again.

"Don't let Hazel undersell herself. It's pretty clear to me that if she cares about teaching even a tenth as much as she cares about anything else she gives her attention to, she's probably easily the best in her district." He shot her a quick grin before seamlessly setting about her next task. "What about you, young lady?" He addressed Elliot's daughter. "What grade are you in, and what do you think of your teacher?"

"It's Zoe," said the young girl, a level of confidence that didn't quite reach Oliver's level but still left something to be desired for Hazel. She should take notes. "I'm in second grade, and my teacher is Mr. Jones. He's not as good as Mrs. Katz, who I had last year, but it's possible I just think that because I'm not as challenged in his class." She sighed dramatically. "Of course, it's possible that is the case because there are way too many naughty kids in that class. If Mr. Jones ever got to do any teaching, I'm sure he would be just fine."

Oliver gave her a knowing nod. "I think we can all relate to that."

Zoe's eyes went wide with understanding. "You can? You mean you had a class clown in your class, too? What did you do to help get the lessons back on track?"

Oliver grimaced, wincing. "I'm afraid it's worse than that, Zoe. I *was* the class clown."

Her sigh was the picture of exasperation. "Well, it seems like that has worked out just fine for you." She gestured around the room. "I'm not sure how it's supposed to help me, though."

Oliver shot a glance at Hazel, something like panic in his eyes. "Any ideas? I could use a little help here."

"Zoe," said Hazel, drawing the girl's attention to herself. "Do you want to know what's really helpful for me when someone in my class is trying to be a clown, trying to distract everyone?"

"Absolutely," said Zoe, leaning forward and tucking her hands under her chin. "What's your secret?"

Hazel had to smile at the precociousness of the little girl. She was sure she was a dream to have in class, and she would have loved—and been kept on her toes at the same time—to have a classroom full of Zoes. "The thing that makes it the hardest, having a class clown, is when everyone else is distracted. It's not about the actual clown, it's about all the laughter and the way everyone has to repeat what the class clown said and just keep carrying on about it. When that happens, I tend to just go stand behind my desk, cross my arms, and wait for everyone to notice that I'm not even trying to teach them."

Zoe nodded sagely. "I've seen that move before. It does seem to work quite well."

"It does. And it's one of those cases where peer pressure can work in a positive way. When the students like you and the other students who actually want to learn something don't laugh at the clown, don't let yourselves get swept up in all the shenanigans, it tends to wrap up much more quickly. You could ask around if there are other students who would like to actually learn, or if that isn't realistic..." She trailed off. It was evident from the way Zoe was nodding that she was, in fact, in the extreme minority in her eagerness to learn second grade world history.

"In that case," said Hazel, "I would recommend talking to Mr. Jones. No doubt, he has noticed the problem, and he can't very well stop trying to create order in the classroom. But he will appreciate knowing that you want to learn, and I bet he would even help you find some extra resources to keep yourself challenged while he tries to reign in the more troublesome students."

Zoe frowned. "Really? That seems like the sort of thing he might find kind of annoying. He would really want me to be reading my own book while he's supposed to be teaching the lesson?"

"I'm almost sure of it," said Hazel. "If you want me to, though, I could write a little note to him. A permission slip of sorts." It would be nothing of the sort, of course. A fellow educator didn't need to be told how to conduct their lessons, but Mr. Jones might get a kick out of knowing just how precocious this student of his was and how exactly she had spent her Christmas vacation talking about curriculum and classroom management. In a classroom full of mixed ability students, she had no doubt that Mr. Jones was already well acquainted with the need to keep the brightest students intellectually stimulated while trying to keep the most talkative students from staging a full-on mutiny.

"Oh, I'm sure I can persuade him," said Zoe. "But you guys can still be pen pals, if you'd like that."

"That's my daughter, ladies and gentlemen," said Elliot, ruffling her hair. "When I tell you she's going to grow up to be an unstoppable force..."

"...I'd say she already is one," finished Oliver, winking at Zoe, who grinned right back at him.

A duo of servers had arrived with trays overloaded with breakfast plates, each of the guests leaning back in turn as the plates were deposited in front of them. As the rest of the table slipped back into their conversations, Oliver leaned towards Hazel.

"You were incredible," he said. "To no one's surprise, of course. Or at least, not to mine."

She scoffed. "It was nothing. At least, nothing I haven't seen in just about every class I've ever taught. The important thing is for the kids whose needs aren't being met to speak up. It surprises me to think that Zoe had managed to keep quiet about her frustrations, but I'm relieved to know that she won't do that now."

Oliver's smile lingered a moment longer before he leaned back to tuck into his plate. The restaurant staff had assembled individual Turkish breakfast plates, they had said, with a little bit of everything on them. There were cheeses and meats, olives and cucumbers and tomatoes, eggs of both the boiled and the fried varieties, and a few small pastries stuffed with various savory fillings.

Hazel began to work her way around the plate, not finishing any one item before moving onto the next one, wanting to be sure she got to taste it all. Once it had all been sampled, she would keep working her way around until she was so full there would be nothing to do about it but sit back, sip another cup of coffee, read a book, and stare out at the sea until her desire to nap was too strong to be resisted.

Daniel cleared his throat and leaned towards her, breaking into her bubble—and away from his phone—for the first time since he had made her introductions. "Did they say what all of this is?" he asked, gesturing to his plate with a knife. "I was checking something on my phone and kind of missed what was going on."

Hazel sniffed, something like a laugh escaping through her nose. "You missed more than just that, Daniel. What was so important, anyway?"

He shrugged. "Just trying to make sure I've got my plans all fleshed out for the next few days. Don't want to miss any of the must-sees, since it's not like I'm going to come back here again."

"You aren't?" She dropped her utensils and turned to look at him. "Why not?"

He looked back at her like she had said something shockingly stupid. "There are too many places to go, Craze. Life's too short to spend it going to the same places for vacation or eating the same things in restaurants. Gotta try it all, or at least as much as you can." He nodded back down to his plate. "So they didn't say what any of this is?"

It was her turn to look at him like he'd just pitched his entry in the Darwin awards. "I think it's pretty self explanatory. You've seen tomatoes and olives before, no doubt." She leaned over to point at the items in turn. "Eggs. Cheese. Sausage."

Daniel sighed. "I know all that. I meant more like the pastries. If they were made with margarine or gluten-free or something like that. Never mind. It doesn't matter." He pushed them aside with his fork and stabbed a cucumber on his fork.

Hazel looked over at Oliver to find him already watching her, and the smile the two of them shared contained unspoken volumes. How was *this* the person at the table she felt most connected to, when her oldest friend felt like he was at least a thousand miles away?

Thirteen

Daniel was the first to stand up when they finished their breakfast. "Right," he began, looking around the table at everyone in turn. "I'm going to head out. If anyone is interested in joining, I'm going to be doing a hike around Göynük Canyon today. It'll be a long one." He looked at Elliot and his family, as if this next part were meant for them. "Probably best just for the serious hikers in the group. So? Anyone interested?"

His question was met with a series of head shakes and polite declining, and he looked at Hazel just a moment longer before nodding. "Alright, Craze. You've got your key? Awesome, then I'll catch you later. No need to wait for me for dinner again tonight."

When he was gone, Hazel sighed. "So much for best friends on vacation across the world." Realizing both Oliver and Anya, Elliot's wife were studying her, she smiled. "Oh, it's fine. Probably best this way. Who really wants to spend the entire day hiking?"

Anya nodded down at her body, and it was only then that Hazel realized she was sitting in a wheelchair. "Oh, I would be all over it," she said, "but I heard it's for serious hikers only." She stuck out her tongue, rolling her eyes, before she turned her attention back to her daughter.

"Oh, for the love..." Hazel leaned towards Oliver, dropping her voice. "Please tell me that isn't what Daniel meant when he looked at their family and ever so subtly implied that they shouldn't join him. I thought he just meant, like...8-year-olds have short legs, you know? I know he can be a bit of a jerk, but not *that* much of a jerk, right?"

"Jerk adjacent, I'd say," said Oliver, tipping his head. "Daniel may unknowingly tread into jerk territory, but he doesn't do it on purpose, and that difference is important." He patted her on the back of the hand. "I'm sure he didn't mean to single out Anya. Daniel...well, he does seem to be the master of obliviousness, doesn't he? We've got to love him for that, I guess."

Hazel shrugged. "Or despite it." She shook her head, clearing the distasteful moment from her awareness. "Anyway. What are you getting up to today? Want some company?"

His smile broadened. "Always. Actually, we were all"—here he gestured around the table—"going to take the shuttle into the city together. Do a bit of exploring and souvenir shopping around the old city and then take the shuttle back again. Does that sound good to you?"

She was already nodding. "Absolutely. I'm dying to see the old city walls, the cliffs...and I definitely need to buy some souvenirs, something for Jack and Claire at the very least. What about you?"

Oliver's eyes changed ever so slightly, like something had passed behind them. "Postcards, for sure. I used to always get a magnet for my grandmother." He huffed out a small chuckle. "Feels strange not to do that, somehow, so I probably still will."

There was a tightening in Hazel's stomach at the mention of Oliver's grandmother. From his words to his overall demeanor, it looked like grief, and even worse, like fresh grief. Tentatively, she bridged the chasm that was so terrifying to her, asking the question she didn't know if he would want to answer.

"You said your grandmother passed away?" At the small nod he gave her, she kept speaking. "Was it very recent?"

"It was." His voice was quiet, only for her ears. "She was fine, healthy as a horse, she used to always say. She had a plane ticket booked, was going to come with me on this trip. Couldn't stop talking about how excited she was." His eyes flashed to Hazel's for just a second before darting away, as if the vulnerability she would see there was too much—or as if, perhaps, he didn't want to break down in tears at the breakfast table. "She was finally going to buy her own magnet, rather than just getting the one I picked out for her. She was so sure there were better magnets out there and that I was holding out on her. But then...well, she just didn't wake up one morning. An aneurysm, the doctor said. It was fast, and she didn't feel any pain. But we felt it all." He swallowed. "I still can't believe she's gone."

"Oh, Oliver." Hazel moved closer to him, wanting to wrap him in her arms but also aware that doing so would attract the sort of attention he definitely didn't want right now, not when he was feeling so raw emotionally. "I'm so sorry," she said. "All this time, you've been listening to me complain about my silly little life, when I should have been listening to you share about your grandma. That changes now. Whatever you need, whatever you want to share about her, I'm here for you. I want to listen and I am happy to hold whatever space you need held."

He put his hand over hers and gave it a quick squeeze. "Thank you, Hazel. If I need to talk, you'll be my first choice. But it isn't as if I've been complaining about the things you want to share with me, is it? If anything, it's been a nice change of pace from all the grief. That's part of why I still came on this trip. I wanted to be around people who would still treat me normally. Back home, everyone is handling me with kid gloves, and it's like they're tiptoeing around things that might upset me. Nobody even says the word 'grandma,' it seems like." He sighed. "It doesn't work like that, though. If anything, it just makes me miss her more, you know?"

Hazel nodded. "Of course. It's, like...well not only do you not have your grandmother with you, but it feels like you aren't even allowed to talk about her."

"Exactly." His eyes were intent on hers, and he looked like he wanted to say something. At the last moment, though, his gaze darted back to the window. "I didn't really expect anyone to understand."

"Ha." The word came out louder than she had intended, a humorless bark. "Well, it just so happens that my particular area of expertise is talking about a person that I miss—though in my case, it's a little different—and the people around me, apart from you, generally not wanting to talk about him. I can't tell you how many times my friends or my brother tried to just not talk about Daniel in an effort to help me 'get over him.'" She held up a hand.

"I know it isn't the same, not at all. And I'm not trying to bring the subject back to me and my fake problems. It's just...it's like these people never heard the saying that absence makes the heart grow fonder, you know?"

"I think they're more focused on 'out of sight, out of mind,'" offered Oliver with his first hint of a smile since he had mentioned his grandma. "That's the beauty of language, I guess. We've got a cliche to cover ever possible experience."

"I guess that's true." Hazel studied Oliver then. "Is there anything I can do for you before we head out?" She looked around the table, their companions all starting to push back their chairs and prepare to leave. "Are we heading out soon, then? No time for a quick walk on the beach first?"

He shook his head. "No, we had better get moving if we don't want them to leave without us. Elliot and Anya arranged for the shuttle to take them since they aren't familiar with the public transportation here and how accessible it may or may not be. In my travel experience, I think that was a good call. People may complain about some places in the US not being accessible enough, but when you start traveling, you can find even more extreme examples. A building that is hundreds of years old might not even have a door that opens wide enough for a large adult to walk in without turning sideways, so no wheelchairs will be fitting in there. And then there are the stairs and hand rails...there's a lot to think about." He shook his head. "Anyway, we'll all be together, and that's good. If we need to muscle Anya's chair up some stairs or over some bumpy terrain, that's what we're all there for."

"For sure," said Hazel, slapping her knees as she pushed up to her feet. "We should get going then. Don't want to be the ones holding up the whole outing, do we?"

The hotel shuttle dropped them all off at the entrance to Kaleiçi, the inner—and older—part of Antalya's downtown. The driver had suggested they could walk down to look at Hadrian's Gate, the typical pedestrian entrance, but that they would struggle with the wheelchair there, given the stairs on either side of it.

"So it begins," said Anya with a game smile, setting off down the sidewalk with her daughter right beside her. "Everything might take a little longer with the chair here," she called over her shoulder, "and I'm not apologizing. Just letting you know."

"There's nothing to apologize about," said Oliver, "unless you happen to be the supreme city planner of all the world and you just forgot to build ramps where they might be needed."

"You know, that is actually not my job title," said Anya, and Hazel could hear the smile in her voice. "But I would be very good at it. If you hear that they're hiring, please do let me know."

"Oh, definitely," said Oliver, smiling down at Hazel. Their group walked a bit further, coming to a stop where the wall of the city turned into three entry arches, the famous Hadrian's Gate the driver had told them about—and that Hazel had read about in the airline's in-flight magazine.

"Wow," she breathed, taking in the structure. "This has been here for almost 2,000 years." She cleared her throat and glanced at Oliver. "I mean, I'm not such a history buff that I just happen to have the ages of every structure around me memorized. I read about it on the way here—on the plane, I mean—and I wanted to take some photos to share it with my students." She lifted up her phone and started snapping pictures. "Would you mind—?" She held out her camera to Oliver, and he quickly began to take more photos of her framed by the ancient gate.

"Together!" cried Zoe, reaching for the phone. "It's better if you take them together. Plus, Hazel looks lonely over there, Oliver." She pushed him bodily towards Hazel. "You should join her."

Oliver sidled into place next to Hazel, a sheepish smile directed her way. "I know your students don't need to see pictures of me," he said in a hushed tone, "but I'm a little scared of Zoe, so I'm just going to follow her directions."

Hazel smiled up at him, then wrapped her arm around his waist. "I don't mind at all," she said. "It'll be nice to have some photos of the two of us, a keepsake to remember my new friend from the trip. I'll text you the best one."

"Er...yeah." Oliver nodded, but his eyes had gone far away. "Thanks."

"Smile, Oliver!" yelled Zoe, shooting a death glare at him over the phone. "And put your arm around Hazel, too. You want this photo to look nice, don't you?"

"Of course I do," he replied, shooting her a broad grin as his arm came to rest around Hazel's shoulder. She relaxed into his touch, only just stopping herself from dropping her head onto his shoulder. Instead, she tightened her grip around his waist and smiled up at him, though his attention remained focused on their tiny photographer. "Look at the camera, Hazel," he said through gritted teeth, not breaking his smile. "She's going to start yelling at you next, if you don't."

"Okay, that's enough," said Zoe, marching forward to hand the phone back to Hazel. "The last ones are the cutest. The way you're looking at him like you're just in love with him." She made a chef's kiss gesture with her small hand. "That's one to frame for sure."

Hazel's laugh surprised her. "Thank you, Zoe."

"You're welcome," the girl replied. "Now, will you take some photos of my family, too?" She called over her shoulder. "Dad! Can you bring your phone here?" Looking back at Hazel and Oliver, she dropped her voice in an almost conspiratorial whisper. "His phone has the best camera."

Once they had taken all the photos they could possibly want, in every combination, they moved away from the gate, further down the sidewalk until they could find a place for Anya's chair to get into the city. She had suggested that she and her family could look for that accessible entrance while the rest of them walked through the gate, reconnecting on the other side, but that had been handily shut down.

"I know this isn't exactly a horror movie scenario," said Oliver, gesturing at the beauty surrounding them. "But I feel like horror movie rules should always apply. And that means we don't separate."

"Plus, we may not all have international plans on our phones," said Austin, their quieter colleague offering an opinion for the first time since at least breakfast. "It's just easier this way."

And with that settled, they all set off, finding the entrance a short distance later and then beginning to explore, wandering up and down the rambling streets of Kaleiçi inside. They stopped to look at textiles, to purchase some fragrant spices, to browse a used bookstore, finally coming to a stop in front of a souvenir store. Oliver waved for the others to go on ahead.

"I just need to pick up something here," he said, "and I need Hazel's help. Why don't you all look for a place to get a coffee or something to eat?"

When they had gone, Hazel looked up at him expectantly. "What am I helping you with?" she asked, looking around at the postcards and miniature spoons on display.

Oliver gestured towards a large display covered in magnets. "One of these, of course." He reached towards a magnet that inexplicably proclaimed "ISTANBUL," with each letter made out of a different cat. "I mean, it should probably be something from Antalya, not that I would be opposed to going to Istanbul sometime."

Hazel nodded as she began to turn the display. "I've heard good things about Istanbul. Should we go there for our next vacation?" It felt good to joke about something so light-hearted with Oliver, and it gave her some kind of unknown thrill to imagine planning a future vacation with him.

"I would love that," he said, and his tone was so sincere that she looked at him in shock. Sure enough, there on his face was a genuine smile, not a hint of playfulness in his eyes. "Just let me know when you're free and I'll be there."

She chuckled softly, playing the whole thing off. "Oh, I will. Just as soon as I scrape together enough pennies for the trip, you'll be the first to know." She picked up a sea turtle magnet and handed it to Oliver. "I like this one. It would be cute on any fridge, this little guy holding up a wedding invitation or a picture of your grandkids. That's got my vote."

"Okay, then," said Oliver without a hint of doubt, heading towards the shopkeeper, sea turtle magnet in hand.

Fourteen

The rest of their day exploring Kaleiçi was lovely. After sitting in a cafe, the adults drinking their various coffees while Zoe tackled a plate of french fries and a lemonade, they made their way to the very edge of the inner city, to the cliff side where the buildings dropped away, leaving only the wide blue sea and the mountains in the distance.

"Wow," breathed Hazel, stopping at the wall to sit and take it all in. The water wasn't the bright turquoise she had imagined the Mediterranean to be, but in the December chill—the air was cool, but the sun was shining—it looked deep and cold and almost icy blue. The mountains behind could have completed the picture if they had been capped with snow. As it was, though, she was glad both that she had put sunblock on before leaving the hotel and that she was wearing a light jacket. If she had brought only her New York winter wear, she would have surely disintegrated into a puddle of sweat by now.

"Do you think Daniel's climbing one of those mountains?" asked Oliver, coming to stand beside her.

Hazel chuckled at the unexpected humor of the question. "I wouldn't put it past him," she admitted. "But really, I have no idea where today's adventures were supposed to take him. We haven't exactly been an open stream of conversation."

"Hmm." Oliver was still looking out at the sea, still focusing his gaze on a distant mountaintop as if he might be able to make out a tiny figure climbing it. "Is that upsetting you?" He glanced down at her for just a second before looking to the distance again.

Hazel sighed. "Oh, Oliver, no. We are not going to do this again." When he gave her a quizzical look, she kept going. "I'm not going to derail our perfectly nice plans and spend the whole day talking about Daniel, and you are not going to listen to me do it." She shook her head. "For what it's worth, no, I'm not upset. We are friends and we will be fine." She gestured around them. "Let's just enjoy this while we can."

"I can get on board with that." Oliver nodded and turned away from the sea with her to take in the path, lined with benches and tall, tall trees. "Does this feel like it's almost Christmas to you?" he asked, nodding towards some bits of garland wrapped around the tall trunks. "Because I have to be honest, I keep forgetting. If I'm not checking the calendar, it's very likely I won't even remember to call my family and wish them a merry Christmas."

"That's a good point." Hazel pulled out her phone, checking the date. "Considering that Christmas is in three days, we're going to have to stay on top of that. I wouldn't go so far as to suggest we make a paper chain to count down the days, but we should at least plan something for the day."

"The Schuler Group is doing a Christmas party. That's on Christmas Eve, though. They're doing another one for New Year's Eve, a week later. We'll be on our own Christmas Day and New Year's Day." He looked at Hazel, an earnestness in his eyes and his words tumbling out rapidly. "Would you like to go with me to the parties? And spend the holidays with me too?" He winced before she could even answer. "That's a big ask, isn't it?"

"Not at all," she said, frowning. "It's not like I have a lot of invitations coming my way and it's greedy for you to ask for all of the days." She leaned towards him, dropping her voice. "I only really have one other friend here, and we both know he is probably going to spend Christmas Day scaling a mountain and then spend New Year's Day accomplishing an entire resolution in one day."

"I think it could be argued that you have more friends than just Daniel and me," said Oliver, gesturing nearby to their companions only to find that Zoe was already watching them, ready with a smile when their eyes met.

"They're all great, aren't they?" Hazel smiled and waved at the little girl before looking back up at Oliver. "I'm not trying to crash a family or a couple's holiday plans, though, even if we *are* staying in the same hotel for the same event. All that to say, I would be thrilled to be your date for any remaining holidays this year. And also to ring in the new year with you."

Oliver grinned at her. "I'm glad to hear it. I have to say, I think it's working out very well for me that Daniel brought you as his plus one. If a more attentive friend had been the one to bring you to Antalya, you would probably be spending all your time with him and we would barely even have met. I think I owe Daniel a bit of appreciation."

Hazel huffed out a laugh. "By that logic, I guess I do too. Must remember to thank him for neglecting me, since it turns out that you're much better company than he is." As soon as she spoke the words, she felt a pang of guilt. "No, I'm not really being fair to him, am I? He's not a bad friend. It's just a complicated situation. Still, we're all making the best of it, aren't we? And what more could we ask for than that?"

"Hmm." Oliver nodded. The peace between them was palpable as they stood side by side taking in the city, the sea, the mountains.

"We're so lucky," Hazel said finally. "It's a good life, and we get to spend a beautiful day like this together, enjoying some really wonderful experiences."

"That's true," said Oliver. And then, quieter and as if he were letting her in on a secret, he continued. "There haven't been a lot of days like this since I lost my grandma. It's not that I felt guilty for having fun or anything like that." He glanced down at her, a small sad smile on his face. "I know some people say they feel that, but I don't think I ever could. Grandma was such a joyful person that it would have taken some real mental gymnastics for me to convince myself she wanted me to spend my days mourning." He sighed. "It's just that without her, and especially with the shock of losing her so suddenly, none of the good stuff felt like it could sink in that deep." He directed his attention to a patch of grass between them and the cliff side that was rippling under the breeze. "The surface level joy was still there, but there was always a gaping hole of sadness underneath it. And it seemed impossible that any of that joy could ever grow big enough to fill even half of that gap."

"You're feeling different now? Being here?" Hazel blinked as she took in his profile, trying to read the lines on his face.

He nodded. "I am. It's like healing, I guess. It doesn't mean it's over, doesn't mean I'm cured and will never feel sad again. But it's easier to believe that I can carry on. That she's still with me in plenty of meaningful ways. And that there's still so much life to enjoy and to live, even if I do it while I'm missing her and trying to learn how to go on. There's a bittersweetness to it, but at least there's sweetness. I'll take bittersweet over numb any day."

"Oh, amen." Hazel hummed. "That's the kind of feeling that lets you know you're alive, doesn't it? It might hurt to lose someone—or in my case, the idea of someone or the hope of something—but if it didn't hurt, then what even was it? If you could lose them and not be devastated, then was it even worth having? I don't know if I'm making sense, but..." She trailed off, discomfort swelling with the awareness that she was performing a soliloquy about grief in front of someone who was in the throes of it. What did she know about grief, anyway, if you didn't count the unique brand of self-inflicted grief where she kept breaking her own heart over and over again by trying to give it to the wrong person?

"You make perfect sense." Oliver looked at her then, really looked at her, and she thought she saw a hint of moisture in his eyes. She dismissed it—the cool breeze coming in from the sea could make anyone tear up—but didn't miss the chance to wrap her arm around Oliver's waist, pulling him next to her until the two of them were once again staring out at the scenery.

Back at the hotel, their little group—their merry band of intrepid adventurers, Elliot had called them, much to his daughter's delight—had dispersed with hugs, laughs, and a promise to do it again before the trip was over. Hazel and Oliver lingered behind, not wanting the moment to end.

"Are we hanging out again soon?" Hazel asked, finally forcing herself to acknowledge that the man might want a moment to himself after spending a full day out in the city.

He tucked his hands in his pockets and shrugged. "You tell me," he said. "I don't exactly have a packed calendar, after all. What are you doing now?"

Hazel shook her head. "You don't want that. You should at least go sit in your room and, I don't know, unwind for a minute. Take a nap or something."

He raised an eyebrow at her. "Do I give off 'needs a nap' vibes? Because if I do, please let me know. I try my hardest not to channel the energy of a toddler or a retiree, and if there's a secret third group I'm not aware of that also loves napping, please let me know so I don't accidentally cosplay as one of them."

Hazel chuckled. "First of all, naps are great, and they are not limited to toddlers and retirees. Have you, for example, considered that there are entire nations who practice the art of taking a siesta? Hmm? For all I know, you could be Spanish or Italian or...hmm..." She lifted her hand to her chin, the picture of wracking her mind. "Oh, right! Or you could be overcoming jet lag, which is the perfect opportunity for someone to take a nap."

"Fair enough. You've made your point." Oliver held up a placating hand. "I am not interested in taking a nap, to answer your question. As it turns out, I am untalented in the art of napping, and if I sleep for even twenty minutes now, then I'll be up all night. I was thinking of grabbing a book from my room and then finding a nice cozy corner of the cafe to read in."

"That sounds great." Hazel smiled at him, silently wishing him the most resting, self-caring afternoon.

"You'll join me then?" When she looked at him, puzzled, he just smiled. "If you somehow understood that as something I wanted to do alone, then you grossly misunderstood. I would absolutely prefer to have you with me. I think it's safe to assume for the rest of this trip that I would always prefer to have you with me."

"Okay, then." Hazel couldn't stop smiling, and she didn't even care that her cheeks were probably burning bright red. Despite the time she had spent with Oliver already on this trip, her old programming still kicked in, assuming that her travel companion would want a break from her company. She had traveled with Daniel enough to know that he regularly wanted time to himself, and she had even learned to enjoy that time. It still felt completely foreign that Oliver would prefer to have her around, even for something as simple as a cup of coffee and a good book.

"I'll meet you back here in five," said Oliver. "I need a minute to decide which book to read."

Hazel blew out a breath in an exaggerated sigh. "You sure that will be enough time? Standing in front of my bookshelf, trying to decide what to read next, is like the equivalent of scrolling through Netflix for 20 minutes before ultimately deciding to just watch Gilmore Girls again."

Oliver winced. "Unfortunately, my selection is quite small. Didn't manage to bring my whole bookshelf with me, but I did decide to only read physical books on this trip. I even left the old Kindle at home."

"What are you choosing between, then? An autobiography of Homer Simpson or an Ikea instruction manual?" she teased.

"Ha ha." He rolled his eyes at her. "It's more like the choice between a nonfiction memoir about death and dying that's sure to be...challenging, shall we say?"

"Or?"

"Or a young adult fantasy novel that my niece has been raving about. If I don't read it, I don't know how I'll even be able to make eye contact with her at the next family gathering." As he spoke, he began to nod. "As I'm saying it out loud, it's all becoming clear. YA fantasy it is. Save the death and dying tearjerker for the plane ride, when I have the opportunity to teach the person sitting next to me that it is, in fact, perfectly acceptable for grown men to cry."

Hazel and Oliver found the perfect booth in the hotel's attached cafe, with an unobstructed view of the sea and baked goods in the display case that the server insisted they take for free along with their lattes, insisting that they were just going to be thrown away at the end of her shift, anyway. Since she wouldn't take any payment for them, they had stuffed even more than the pastries were worth into the tip jar on the counter, sitting in the booth side by side so that they could share the view of the sea.

Sitting and reading in silence was transcendental. Hazel lost herself in the pages of Claire's new book, feeling the need to almost physically remove herself from the romantic setting of the story as she blinked up and out at the water before sneaking a glance at Oliver beside her, a smirk playing across his lips as he read the adventure novel his niece had loved so much.

Normally, when Hazel read a romance novel, the stark contrast between the depictions on the page and her everyday life could create a bit of ennui or even sadness. She would read about the hero and his grand gesture, the tender vulnerability he showed to win over his leading lady, and then she would look at the unanswered messages she had sent Daniel. She would then have to do mental gymnastics to convince herself yet again that the two of them were, somehow, still meant to be together, that this was all part of the grand plan of what was going to make their love story so beautiful when it finally shifted from friends to lovers in that most favorite trope of hers.

But today, as she was reading Claire's sweet love story, looking up to find herself in the real world with Oliver didn't create the sort of cognitive dissonance she was used to. She read about a man on the page who was strong and capable and who had a softer side...and then she looked to her right to find a man who had all the same traits and then some.

It wasn't as if she believed she and Oliver were a couple or that there was even the potential of any real romantic interest on his part. She certainly wouldn't explore her own feelings on the matter—didn't dare to, in fact, if she wanted to preserve any sense of pride she might have. But, for the first time, she admitted to herself that if he really were interested, if he were to ask her out for a date that wasn't just intended to be an ego boost or something to help her move on...she knew what her answer would be. She would be so lucky to have him in that capacity, and that was exactly why she couldn't let herself imagine it.

Better to imagine the man I know is going to break my heart in that role, she thought, *than to dare to hope for one who might not. Stick to what you're good at, kid.*

Fifteen

It was almost too easy for Hazel and Oliver to decide to stay at the hotel for dinner. Between all the sunshine and walking of the day, they decided they were both too tired to put in the effort of changing their clothes and going out in search of something new.

"Besides," Hazel offered, "it's still new to us. It's not like we've eaten dinner here at the hotel yet."

"That's true," said Oliver, leaning towards her to drop his voice. "Also, don't tell anyone else, but I'm not exactly keeping score of all the cool places I eat on this trip. If I don't eat in every Instagram-famous restaurant Antalya has to offer or even if I stay in my room and order a hamburger, I'm still going to consider this trip perfect."

Hazel scowled at him. "That sounds like borderline Daniel slander, since you know that is not his approach to travel at all." Now it was her turn to lean closer, as if her next words were a secret. "But I won't tell him if you don't."

"Good to know, but it was actually nothing to do with Daniel," said Oliver. "Just my personal philosophy. So on that note...we are choosing to eat in the restaurant, right? I can't tempt you into coming over to my place for some room service?"

Surely, her cheeks were heating, and the only way she could even think to camouflage that fact was to shake her head so vigorously that he couldn't focus on one of them at a time. "No, let's go to the restaurant," she said. Why was it that the thought of being invited into Oliver's room made her feel so scandalized? True, she hadn't actually been inside it, but would their relationship be altered so fundamentally by the simple act of closing a door behind them?

It must be about the fact that a hotel room, even one as luxurious as the ones they were staying in, was a glorified bed room. Oh, there was a desk to sit at, and even an extra arm chair. But nothing could alter the fact that there was a giant bed there, too. Two, in fact, if his room was arranged the same as Hazel and Daniel's was.

Not that Hazel was thinking about Oliver in his bed. Not that she wanted to think about Oliver in his bed. In fact, she pointedly wanted to avoid thinking about Oliver in his bed, and that was why she couldn't be in a room with him that had such a complete lack of other conversation pieces. She could visit a furniture warehouse with him. Maybe even arrange a trip to Ikea. The mere presence of couches and sinks and refrigerators kept everything safely in familiar territory. For now, all she could do was say no to visiting the room where he slept and try not to make it weird.

"It's just that, in the restaurant, if we decide we want something more, we're right there, you know? If we order room service and it turns out everything is, like, microscopic proportions or the fries are all cold, then we'd have to order again and wait again." She shrugged. "In an ideal world, it could work, but right now it feels like a gamble."

Oliver nodded as if her words had been sage wisdom and not the incoherent ramblings of a woman who didn't quite know how she felt about him. "That makes sense to me," he said. "We'll have a pajama party some other time, then."

They both tucked their books into Oliver's messenger bag, with Hazel making stunted jokes about the role reversal of a man being the one carrying a bag for a change.

"Daniel was always asking me to put his phone in my purse, back when we were in high school. It used to drive me nuts," she said, immediately regretting bringing Daniel up again as soon as she had. The uncomfortable feeling she got in her gut every time she thought about her friend, about the gulf between them, and about her uncertainty that her new focus on spending time with Oliver was only widening the gulf even further when she should have been trying her darnedest to repair it.

"I'm happy to hold on to your book for you," said Oliver. "Just in case you were worried I felt like you did in high school."

They entered the restaurant, which was now missing the friendly welcome committee Mr. Schuler and his grandchildren had provided in the morning. Instead, there was a sign encouraging them to find their own seats and wait to be served, so they did just that.

As Oliver led the way to a small table near the fireplace—Hazel was thrilled to see the flames dancing in it, and to hear faint jazzy Christmas melodies playing over the sound system—she spotted Mr. Schuler's daughter sitting by herself, looking down into a glass with the saddest expression on her face.

Hazel, who had been following Oliver at a pace, closed the distance between them and grabbed his hand and his attention. She tilted her head subtly in the direction of Mr. Schuler's daughter at the confused look he gave her, and she watched as understanding dawned on him. His confusion melted into something that looked like concern, and he pulled Hazel—who was inexplicably still holding his hand—closer to him as he dropped his voice.

"Newly a widow," he breathed. "I imagine the holidays are hard for her."

Hazel closed her eyes as she took in his words, her heart breaking for the very real pain this young mother must be feeling. "We should check on her, right?" she asked, looking up at him. "You know grief, Oliver. Would you want that?"

"I..." His eyes bounced between hers as he seemed to contemplate something before he finally nodded. "I wouldn't, actually. Not from most people. But from you? Always."

"Okay, then." She steered him in a new direction then, towards Mr. Schuler's daughter's table.

"Er..." she began when the woman looked up at her, only in that moment realizing she didn't know the woman's name.

"Nora?" Oliver stepped forward, saving the day with his foreknowledge of the most valuable piece of information, the mystery woman's name. "Would you mind if we joined you? Just for a moment?" He nodded towards her empty glass. "A beverage, perhaps?"

Nora looked puzzled, her eyes tracking between Oliver and Hazel, settling for a moment on where their hands were clasped together. She cleared her throat as she seemed to put herself back together, a smile appearing on her face that didn't reach her eyes. "It's Oliver, right?" At his nod, her gaze moved to Hazel. "And this is your...wife? Girlfriend?"

How different did it feel to be mistaken for Oliver's partner than it had just that morning when she had been mistaken for Daniel's? Hazel almost nodded, wanting only to indulge the fantasy for a moment longer, but Oliver was already speaking.

"This is Hazel," he said. "A good friend of mine."

"Nice to meet you, Hazel," said Nora, giving her a smile and nodding towards the empty seats at her table. "Would you two like to join me?"

As they sat down, Hazel couldn't stop herself from hurrying to explain their presence. "It's not...we aren't here to, I don't know, talk about work or anything. It's just..." She sighed. "I'm so sorry. This might be totally inappropriate. But Oliver told me that you're recently widowed, and well, he and I have been talking about grief and loss a lot, and I just couldn't stand the thought that maybe no one was giving you the space to talk if maybe that was what you needed. To talk. To not have to pretend to be okay."

Nora blinked rapidly, her gaze fixed on Hazel, until finally a couple of stray tears fell down her cheeks. "Damn," she said. "I really needed someone to say that." She turned her attention to Oliver. "She's a good one, Oliver. Don't let her go." That statement brought on a fresh wave of tears, and the three of them sat together as the emotion moved through Nora.

"I'm sorry," she finally said, a new smile on her face, but one that felt more real this time, even framed by her two sad eyes. "I know most people don't know how to be around someone who is grieving, and I don't blame them. I'm sure I said my fair share of platitudes and nonsense when I was the uncomfortable one sitting where you're sitting."

"Not at all," said Oliver, giving her a kind smile. "I recently lost my grandmother, so I can sit with you as long as you need someone to." And then, just when Hazel was starting to worry that her presence there might be redundant, he reached his hand over to hers and gave it a squeeze. "And Hazel has been better at being with me in that grief than anyone outside my family has been. For tonight, or for however long you need, we're here for you."

She was blinking rapidly again, dabbing at the spots beneath her eyes. "That's very kind of you both," said Nora, reaching for her empty glass. "And I may take you up on it again. For tonight, at least, I should get back to my children. I'm sure my parents are sick of cartoons by now, and it's not like the kids aren't going through grief of their own, like they don't need their mother there, too." She squeezed both of their hands. "Thank you both, again, for the renewal of my faith in humanity, not to be too dramatic about it." She pushed back her chair and rose to her feet. "I wouldn't say I was sitting here feeling sorry for myself. I know, after all, how hard it is to be a widow. But I was definitely sitting here feeling like if it weren't for my kids and for my parents, I don't think I would want to live in a world without Thomas." She held up a hand to answer the question they hadn't asked. "That's not a cry for help. That's just the desperate sadness of losing your most perfect partner. Anyway, you two showed me kindness, and if I believed in that kind of thing, I would think that Thomas had sent you. Thank you. Truly."

She pressed her hands to her chest, her eyes still shining, before she turned and left the restaurant and the two of them in her wake.

"Wow," was all Hazel could say.

"Yeah," agreed Oliver. "That's really hard stuff, what she's going through." He squeezed Hazel's hand, only making her aware in that moment that their palms were still clasped together. "I'm glad you listened to your intuition and brought us over to her."

"Me, too. I wish there was more we could do."

He nodded. "Sometimes just being there is enough. Or at least it's a good start."

That dinner felt like it had shifted things between them, like it had continued to tilt Hazel's world and all its orbiting moons on its axis. The companionable silence she shared with Oliver seemed to deepen in its understanding with every day, or even with every meal, of this trip.

And it wasn't as if it was all silence. There was plenty that they laughed about, plenty of random thoughts to share and subsequent rabbit trails to follow, plenty of hot takes on the current events that flashed on the screen of a nearby silent television.

But the silence was what mattered most to Hazel. The silence between two people was so often the moment for anxieties to flare, for her to second guess what she could have done to cause it. Had she not asked the right questions? Was she too boring? Did she need to be more, better, different to keep things flowing the way they were supposed to?

It was one of the biggest struggles of her early days as a teacher, learning to be comfortable with a certain amount of silence. Not that silence was a particularly common occurrence in her elementary school classroom. But being comfortable with her own silence, particularly after she asked her students a question, was a skill that she had honed only after lots and lots of practice.

It was human nature to fill silence, and it was human nature for a brand new teacher to ask a question, and, if it was not answered immediately, to either rephrase the question or ask follow-up questions, or give hints or just outright answer the question. Her mentor teacher, from her very first day in her student teaching classroom, had drilled into Hazel's mind the need to wait. It was only when she allowed that white space to stretch that some of the more reluctant students would even dare to speak.

It had been an excruciating lesson to learn, and it had colored much of Hazel's interaction with her peers and friends and dates after that time, too. On a first date with an acquaintance of Jack's, she found herself counting the seconds of silence, which quickly turned into tallying an inner chart to determine whose fault the silence was. Even though part of her could admit that her date had asked just as few engaging questions as she had, she couldn't help but infer that it was her fault that things weren't flowing.

All of it made her appreciate the silences she shared with Oliver even more. She wasn't weighing what to say next and how he might react to it, like she sometimes did with Daniel. She wasn't even swept away in her racing thoughts, worrying about her lesson plans and her classroom decorations for St. Patrick's Day at the same time like she sometimes did when she was with her brother. She was, instead, simply taking in the moment. The beautiful gleam of the moon on the sea across the street, the delicious interplay of rich lamb, tangy yogurt, tomato sauce, warm bread, and sizzling butter of the dish—İskender kebap—she and Oliver had both ordered. All in all, it was the closest thing in recent recollection to a completely blissful, peaceful moment.

"That was as delicious as anything we would have eaten out at a restaurant," declared Oliver as he arranged his silverware on his empty plate. "And it spared us a walk, too. That's a win in my book."

Hazel groaned. "Speak for yourself. I still have to walk back to my room, and right now that sounds like a near physical impossibility." She peered around the nearly empty restaurant. "Do you think they would let me sleep in one of the booths here?"

He leveled a glare at her, but he chuckled softly, too. "You'll be fine. The walk will be good for your digestion, and I'm sure you'll sleep like a log."

Hazel pulled a face. "Whatever that even means." She looked around for their server. "This one is on me tonight." She pointed a finger at Oliver. "No arguing, and don't you even dare tell me you already asked for it to be charged to your room when you went to the bathroom."

He held up his hands. "Tonight, I didn't do any of that. And I won't argue, either. If you want to buy me meat, you are welcome to buy me meat. As much as I enjoy feeding you, I can accept that you might want to get a chance to do the same."

"That's a weird way of putting it." Hazel rolled her eyes. "But thank you."

After paying the bill and saying goodnight to Oliver, she made her way to her room, slipping her key into the door to let herself in the door with a big smile still on her face from the evening.

When the door opened, though, her smile faltered. Daniel was sitting on his bed, looking for all intents and purposes like an anxious parent waiting for his wayward child to return from a raucous party. Her pulse picked up and she swallowed.

"Daniel? What's going on?"

Sixteen

"I'm glad you're back, Craze." Daniel shook his head. "We need to talk."

Her stomach dropped as she sat down next to him on the edge of the bed, her mind already racing with any number of worst-case scenarios. Had something happened to her family? His family? Had something happened out on his hike today? Oh, why couldn't he just come right out with it and tell her the worst of it?

"What's going on, Daniel?" she asked, panic in her voice. "What happened? Is someone hurt? Sick?" She gulped. "Is it worse than that?"

He startled, recoiling, as he turned to look at her. "No, nothing like that. Why would you even think that?"

Hazel sighed, equal parts relieved and growing furious that he could be that oblivious. "Well, you're sitting here in silence like you're waiting to stage an intervention, and then you tell me we need to talk with that serious look on your face. I don't know what else I'm supposed to think." She crossed her arms over her chest and turned, refusing to look at him.

Daniel let out an exaggerated sigh. "I didn't mean it like that, Craze, and I'm sorry if you took it that way. But the fact is that we do need to talk." He bumped his shoulder into hers, prompting her only to pull further away, not to loosen up as he had intended.

"And what do we need to talk about?" she asked, tilting her head the bare minimum to sneak a glance at him. She was pleased to see he looked contrite, even if it was only the barest amount.

"I'm sure you've noticed that things have been...strained...with us. And I don't like it. We need to fix it."

Hazel let out a humorless laugh. "Is it that easy, Daniel? You just...fix it? How? Do you even know what's wrong between us?"

He frowned at her. "Of course I do." He gestured between them. "It's, you know, the whole *feelings* thing. You have these feelings for me, and I don't have them, and that makes things weird and awkward."

"Uh, huh. And how do you propose we fix that, exactly?"

Daniel shrugged. "Well, I don't know that, not really. I mean, if you could stop having the feelings, that would probably be the best option. I'm sure that's not really possible though, since, you know, I'm the supreme catch that I am." He bumped his shoulder into hers again, turning his face to hers with such a cheesy grin that she, eventually, couldn't help but let out a laugh.

"I'm working on it, Daniel," she said. "Believe it or not, it's not actually that much fun for me to carry these feelings around like the world's worst mismatched luggage set." As she said the words, something dawned on her. The feelings that she claimed to be carrying around, that she had assumed she must still feel simply because they had been her constant companions so long...when she felt around in her psyche for them, she couldn't locate them.

There was something else—or perhaps *someone* else—that was taking up a lot more space, though.

She turned to Daniel, excited at what she had just learned. "Actually," she breathed. "I think something might have changed. I don't feel the same way I did before. Not really." She paused for a moment as if trying to feel something, then shook her head. "No, it's not the same. I wouldn't cry myself to sleep if you went out on a date with someone." Her eyes widened as she grabbed his shoulder. "You should go out on a date with someone."

Daniel frowned. "W-what? What are you talking about, Craze? How could you change, just like that?"

Hazel shrugged, struggling to translate her excitement into words. "I don't know...not really. Maybe it's about all this time I'm spending with Oliver. He's been a really good friend to me, and I think...well, it almost feels like that's healing something."

"So that's it then, you just find someone else?" Daniel's lip had twitched into a sneer. "So you aren't holding onto hope about me because you found another guy? And, worst of all, it's him?" He shook his head. "I don't understand you, Craze. Is your taste really so...varied? How could the same girl who liked me for ten plus years be into him?"

Her excitement had been replaced with something that resembled the beginnings of rage. "He's a good man,

Daniel. And for your information, I am not talking about having feelings for Oliver. That's not what it is. He's just...well, maybe it's shocking for me to have a man as a friend who's actually being a good friend to me. Not one who's taking every opportunity he has to avoid me or call me a belittling nickname or act like he's actually offended when people confuse us for being a couple."

"Wow." Daniel nodded once. "Didn't realize you felt that way about our friendship."

Hazel's sigh was the dictionary definition of exasperation. "I don't, you big idiot! You're my best friend, and I care about you, and I think we have a lot of fun together. I just...I wish you would stop acting like such a jerk just to keep me at arm's length. Anyone and everyone who sees us together is just going to get the wrong idea about you and, by extension, the wrong idea about me."

"What do you mean?" His face was the picture of confusion.

Hazel pursed her lips, plowing ahead in her explanation. "I mean that every time you call me *Craze*, you paint yourself as the kind of guy who's a little bit cruel. And in turn, that paints me as the kind of girl who's so desperate for male attention that she'll take any of it, even if it is cruel." She put her hand on his. "We're better than that, aren't we?"

"Of course we are," he huffed. "And you know I don't like acting like this. That I wish I could just go back to being a teddy bear."

"I know, Daniel." She patted his hand. "For what it's worth, you've been doing a really great job acting in this role. But that'll do, pig. That'll do."

"Hey." He recoiled, mock offense on his face. "If I can't call you Craze anymore, then I hardly think you should be calling me pig." He looked serious when his eyes found hers then. "So can we really do it, go back to the way we were before? I don't want to make things hard for you. You think you can handle me being Charming Daniel again without getting ideas about love and marriage and a baby carriage?"

She hit him lightly on the arm. "I think I've got more than enough Jerk Daniel nightmare fuel to keep me away from that particular day dream." She pressed her lips into a line. "But if that changes, I promise I'll tell you. Give you full permission to unleash the beast again."

Daniel winced. "I really was a beast, wasn't I?"

"I mean..." She grimaced. "Do you want the truth?"

"Not really." He shook his head and then let out a sigh. "Well, at least I still have some time to repair my reputation here with the rest of my coworkers. Really turn on the charm." He wiggled his eyebrows at her. "Maybe even meet someone."

"You should," she said, and she was surprised that she meant it. "I think finding yourself a date for New Year's Eve might be just what the doctor ordered."

"You mean with one of my coworkers?" Daniel's eyes were comically wide now, and she laughed.

"I'm not giving you permission to make things messy at work, so don't even try to blame it on me if that's exactly what you do." She shrugged. "Just...I don't know. Be open to whatever might happen next."

He bumped her shoulder one more time. "Is that what you're doing? With Oliver, I mean?"

"I don't know," she admitted. "I'm trying not to replace having a crush on one of my friends with having a crush on another of my friends…don't want to be a cliche, after all." She lifted her shoulders. "But at least I'm being reminded that there are other men out there."

"Good ones," said Daniel. "Oliver is a really, really good one. It was definitely not the highlight of my trip so far, trying to pretend that I thought he was a jerk."

Hazel frowned. "Then why did you do that?"

"Had to lean into the full persona of the thing, Haze. Make myself as unlikeable as possible. I sort of figured it might drive you into his arms, the two of you mutually hating on me. Also really leaned into my whole gym bro identity and found out it is not for me." He winced as he extended his legs in turn in front of him. "I'm taking a rest day tomorrow for sure. Maybe a rest week, actually. Believe it or not, there is such a thing as too much hiking."

She had to laugh at that. "Oh, I am well aware of that fact. And I'm glad to hear that you are too now, apparently."

"Definitely." He was silent for just a beat before glancing at her. "So, we're good then?"

She nodded. "We're good. Better than I ever expected, actually." She gave him her broadest grin. "It's good to have you back, bud."

"It's really good to have you back, too, Haze." He flung his arm around her shoulders and pulled her in for a quick side hug.

♥ • ♥ • ♥ • ♥ • ♥

The following morning, Hazel nearly skipped out of bed, she was in such a hurry to see Oliver. Her conversation the night before with Daniel had given her the clarity about what was really in her heart, at least as far as any potential relationships were concerned, and all she wanted now was to see the man who was on her mind.

"Slow down, Haze," said Daniel, holding her purse out to her before she could escape out the door of the room. "You don't want to forget this, do you?"

She sighed, grabbed the purse, then headed back to the door. "I can just meet you there. Save you a seat."

"Not so fast." He grabbed the door before it could swing closed. "I don't know where you think you're going without me, but you're not as fast as you think. I'm literally right behind you."

"Fine. Just walk fast."

In the restaurant, she spied Oliver right where she had expected to find him, sitting at the same table as the morning before, with all the rest of their companions from the previous breakfast.

"You should get to know the others today," she told Daniel in a low voice. "Now that you aren't playing Jerk Daniel, I mean. I'm sure they would all appreciate getting to know you. And Anya might like to know that you aren't actually an ableist jerk who wanted the lady in the wheelchair to know she wasn't welcome to tag along on his little hike."

Daniel's face paled as he looked at her with wide eyes. "I didn't even know she was in a wheelchair." His hand flew up to cover his mouth. "Did I really look right at her when

I said something about the hike being for serious hikers only? I swear I didn't know, and I would never..."

Hazel put a hand on his arm. "I mean, I know all of that, but I'm sure she would appreciate hearing it from you, too. And, of course, the best apology is changed behavior. Maybe today you could spend some time with your coworkers rather than disappearing to do all your strong man stunts by yourself."

Daniel groaned. "Don't remind me. I slept well last night, but as soon as I woke up, it's like all the sore muscles came back with a vengeance. It's taking every ounce of my will to not start hobbling down this hall right now."

"Too much pride to admit you may have been wrong?" She raised an eyebrow at him.

"Something like that," he said.

By then, they had reached the table, greeting their companions there as Oliver got to his feet to give Hazel a quick embrace and Daniel a nod.

"Hey, man," said Daniel to Oliver as he sat down. "Good morning. Nice to see you again."

Oliver gave Hazel a puzzled glance, but she just shook her head. "I can explain later," she whispered, turning to watch Daniel's next move.

Sure enough, he wasted no time in engaging the rest of the table. "Good morning, Thompsons," he greeted Austin and his wife. "Elliot," he said with a nod. "Zoe, how is your trip going so far? Anya, are you enjoying Turkey?"

The others blinked at him, as if processing this change in his personality, but Zoe jumped right into her response. "It's really good," she said. "We had so much fun in the city yesterday. Have you been there yet? You should really go."

She turned to her mom, a spark in her eyes. "We should go again too, shouldn't we, Mom? We can bring some cat treats to feed the cats and we can buy some towels for Grandpa. Oh, can we go, Mom? Please?"

"We'll see, Zoe," said Anya, tipping her head towards the others. "I'll need at least another adult with us for a little help on the uneven streets. We'll have to ask your dad what he's got planned for today, but maybe you can talk him into it."

"I'd be happy to join you," Daniel offered. "Zoe is right, and I definitely shouldn't miss what the city has to offer." He rubbed the back of his neck. "I've definitely been a little overly ambitious with all the hiking, and I'm about ready to give it a rest, to be honest."

"That's nice," said Anya with a sniff. "Let's discuss it after breakfast."

When they all had their breakfast—the restaurant had resumed its normal operations and the meal was served buffet-style today—Oliver leaned over to speak into Hazel's ear. "Is it my imagination, or did Daniel have some kind of personality transplant overnight?"

She smiled at him. "We had a conversation last night. A good one, actually. I think you'll be seeing this version of him from here on out."

"New and improved Daniel?" he asked with a lifted eyebrow.

"It's more like the old, classic Daniel. This is who he used to be all the time before he apparently decided acting like a jerk might be the best strategy for getting me to stop having feelings for him."

Oliver's eyes widened at her words. "Oh. Wow. I mean...that's one strategy, I guess." He studied her for a moment. "So...he's not doing that anymore?"

Hazel shook her head as she speared a piece of cheese on her fork. "He's not. It's not necessary anymore, as it turns out."

"Oh? Uh...why not?" He was tracking the movement of her utensils on her plate, as if he couldn't quite bring himself to meet her eyes.

"I guess we don't need that jerky behavior to create a buffer between us anymore." She shrugged.

Oliver's eyes darted to hers. "Did something happen last night? Are you two—?"

Hazel chuckled as she grasped his meaning. "Oh, no. Not even a little. It's pretty much the opposite, actually." She lifted the cheese to her lips, chewing slowly as she watched his face. "It seems like I just don't really have those feelings for him anymore. Like...well, like I've moved on, I guess."

He frowned. "Oh yeah? But...how? What happened? And why didn't you say anything?"

"I didn't realize it until the moment. It was...well, it was a bit strange. It was like I was looking for the feelings inside myself, in the place where I always keep them...but they just weren't there." She looked into his eyes, blinking. "And I think I have you to thank for that?"

Confusion clouded his features. "Me? What did I do?"

She reached over, patting his hand. "Don't worry about it right now, Oliver. We'll talk soon, I promise."

Seventeen

Hazel had told Oliver she was going to need a little time on her own that morning to catch up on a few things. Daniel had left after breakfast with Elliot's family, a broad smile on his face as Zoe slipped her hand into his and steered him towards the shuttle.

When she had the room to herself, she flopped onto the bed, staring up at the ceiling. There was so much swirling in her mind, so many thoughts and feelings that she couldn't quite get them all to fall into line. She was relieved to have things back to normal with Daniel, and she was eager to share everything with Oliver...and yet, something was holding her back at the same time.

As she stared, her version of meditation that looked much more like ruminating on anxiety-inducing thoughts, she remembered the days before she had first confessed her feelings for Daniel. They had felt much the same as this moment did right now, full of possibility and hope. She had believed then that all Daniel needed to hear was that she loved him for him to unlock those same feelings inside himself.

She sat bolt upright as she recognized that same feeling in the present moment. There was a not insignificant part of her that believed everything was about to change for the better. That she was going to take Oliver aside, tell him she had feelings for him, and that was going to be the turning point of their relationship for the rest of their lives.

Even as she thought it, she cringed. If experience had taught her anything, it was that feelings were at least as likely to be unreciprocated as they were to be shared. But the other, more significant thought that was making her wince at her reflection in the mirror was the predictability of her heart, her feelings, her emotions.

It had only been days since she had felt these feelings with Daniel as their target. Now, that target had shifted to Oliver—she was finally admitting that to herself—but did that really mean there was something special between them? Or did that just mean that she was physically incapable of not carrying a torch for someone?

Hazel groaned as she reached for her phone. Checking the time and doing some quick mental math, she noted that it was 2am in New Jersey. Still, she gritted her teeth, hoping her brother was smart enough to turn off his phone if he was asleep, and sent a quick text message.

"Jack, I know it's super late there, but on the off chance that you're up, can we chat?"

She tossed the phone away, groaning as she lay back on the bed. Not only was her brother unlikely to be awake at this hour, but he was even less likely to be looking at his phone. No, if she knew him at all—and she certainly should after more than two decades as siblings—

Hazel was interrupted from her thoughts by the sound of her phone vibrating next to her head. She jolted upright with it in hand, an incoming video call from her older brother.

"Well, huh. Shows how much I know, I guess..." she said as she swiped the screen to accept the call.

"Hazel!" Jack's face filled the screen. The room was dark, and his eyes looked tired, but he was grinning broadly.

"Hi, big bro," she said, her own smile mirroring his. "What in the world are you doing up at this hour?"

"Oh, right. You know Claire's whole Christmas Eve Eve thing?"

Hazel nodded, remembering Claire's tradition of spending the night before Christmas Eve with her best friend, Emma, watching as many Christmas movies as they possibly could before parting ways to spend the holiday with their respective families.

"Well, Emma is here. She's on a completely different time zone, and the two of them are just about out of their minds with the joy of being reunited. Between all the talking about wedding planning and the sheer volume of movies they're convinced they need to watch, it seems unlikely that anyone is going to be getting much sleep tonight."

Hazel smiled. She would have liked to be there with them, to get to meet Claire's friend, Emma, who lived in Ireland and was planning a wedding there the following summer. "Sounds like a blast," she said, meaning it. "One of these years, I'm going to crash your Christmas Eve Eve party."

"And you would be so welcome!" she heard Claire call from out of the frame. "It's an open invitation, Hazel dear."

Jack smiled in the direction the voice had come from, then made to leave the room. "You two keep watching without me," he said off-camera. "I'm going to go chat with Hazel for a bit."

"Sorry, Jack. I don't mean to keep you," she said when the door of his bedroom closed behind him.

He waved her concern away. "Please. I don't need to see it happen every time an uptight career man or woman falls for their small-town love interest and learns the true meaning of Christmas in order for me to know that's exactly what's going to happen. I do refuse to miss it when they put *Die Hard* on, though. We might even watch it in German again just for old times' sake."

Hazel chuckled. "You and your traditions."

Jack raised his eyebrows and nodded. "Me and my traditions. Anyway, what's going on with you? How's Turkey? And what's on your mind?"

Hazel sighed. "I'm good and Turkey is good. I think a little break from the cold and gray back home is just what the doctor ordered. Seeing the sun in December is surprisingly soothing to the soul."

"I'm sure it is, even if I can't begin to imagine it." Jack smiled. "Are things okay with Daniel? Claire and I have been worried about you, hoping the two of you were having a nice time and that it wasn't doing too much of a number on your heart." He winced then. "I have to admit, when you talked about a Christmas getaway, I liked the idea a lot more before I knew Daniel was going to be there with you. Awfully hard to get over someone when you're looking at their face every day."

She nodded. "Normally, I would agree with that, but actually, Daniel is the least of my worries right now. Oh, he made everything worse for a while, apparently deciding that he should be a jerk to me and everyone else in some valiant effort to help me stop having feelings for him."

"Yikes." Jack visibly recoiled. "Please tell me you put an end to that."

"It's over now," she confirmed. "Partly because I realized I just don't feel the same way towards him anymore." She raised her eyebrows to match her brother's expression, eagerly awaiting his reaction.

"You...what? But how? And are you sure?"

"Pretty sure, yeah. I just...well, I've been spending time with the other guy. Oliver. I told you about him. He's been a really good friend. I guess part of it is that when I compare the way he treats me compared to the way Daniel always has, it's just so obvious that Daniel was never going to see me as anything but a friend."

Jack nodded. "I'm glad to hear you say that. And this other guy? Oliver? What are the vibes there? Could it be something other than friendship?"

Hazel leaned against her headboard as she let out a sigh. "That's the thing that's bugging me. I don't even want to go there, Jack. I mean...I do, but also I don't, you know?"

He shook his head. "I don't actually have the first idea what you mean by that. Why wouldn't you want to go there? Is he a good guy?"

She nodded. "He's great. So kind, so easy to be around...just...yeah. Great."

Jack pressed his lips together. "Ah. Got it. You're not attracted to him." He held up a hand. "Believe it or not, I don't really need to hear more about that. The less I know about what physical male characteristics my little sister considers attractive, the better."

She was blushing now. "It's not that. The opposite, actually. Oliver is *very* attractive."

Jack just blinked. "Then I fail to see the problem."

"It's not about him, Jack. It's about me. How much of a cliche am I that I just trade in having a crush on one guy for having a crush on another? It's embarrassing. I don't think I could even admit this to anyone but you."

"What...what exactly is the problem, Haze? You feel like you're jumping too quickly from one crush to another?" He raised a single brow.

"Well, yeah. You see how people talk about it when an actress or a singer jumps from one boyfriend to another, everyone always criticizing her for not being able to be single."

"Uh, yeah. I see that, and I see how rarely those same comments are directed at men who do the same thing," Jack said, his eyes conveying the depth of his sincerity. "So if this is all some fear of misogynistic judgment, then I think it's time to let it go."

"But isn't there some truth to it?" she asked. "I mean, don't I need to be alone? To be okay on my own?"

Jack sighed. "Haven't you *been* alone this whole time? Was it ever really you and Daniel in a relationship, or was it just a relationship that existed only in your mind? When she was silent, he continued. "If you had actually been a couple, and certainly if you had been together for the decade plus that you've had these feelings for him, then yeah. I'd say you should take a break before jumping right into something else." He shook his head. "But this is different, Haze. It's the difference between you keeping yourself safe by only giving your heart away to someone who was never going to take it, certainly never going to treasure it. Now, the difference is that you're directing your sights on someone who, from the sounds of it at least, is a lot more likely to accept that gift and to treat you the way you deserve to be treated. I don't think you need to wait any longer to see what that feels like, to be in a relationship, to let yourself be loved rather than always being the one who is loving."

Hazel was quiet a moment longer as she processed his words. When she spoke again, her voice was small. "What if I'm wrong? What if it just ends up being more of the same, another man who doesn't actually see me like that and just wants to be my friend? What if I get hurt again?"

"You might." Jack nodded. "Getting hurt is always a possibility when it comes to love and vulnerability. And I don't know this Oliver, so I certainly don't know what his feelings are for you."

"Then why do you seem so sure that this could be different?"

He nodded towards her. "Because of you. Because of how different you seem. Not only have you let go of something that you carried around for ten years, but, even through the nerves that you're clearly feeling, there's a change there. A confidence. Something about you that seems to suggest that you're being cared for and appreciated just as you are and that's giving you a little self-esteem boost that, may I just say, is long overdue? You've been try-ing to contort yourself to be whatever you thought Daniel might want you to be for so long, and it seems like you aren't doing that anymore." His shrug was nonchalant. "I think, no matter what happens with this Oliver, it's worth it to talk to him about your feelings and see what his are. No matter what, it'll be good to clear the air. See what might happen. And even if nothing does happen, this will be different than it has been with Daniel. You don't even ever have to see this guy again after your trip is over, so it's not like it's going to be the awkwardness of still being best friends and seeing each other all the time."

Hazel's stomach twisted. "I don't want to not see him again after this trip is over."

Jack gave her a knowing nod. "Then that sounds like all the more reason to talk to him. Do it, Haze. Be brave. It will be worth it."

"If you're sure." She pushed her lips together. "Could you run it by Claire, too? I'd feel better if I knew you both were on the same page."

"Get out of here." Jack laughed. "I'll have you know there is more than one relationship expert in this relation-ship, and if Claire were sitting here with me, she would be nodding right along with everything I'm saying." He glared at her across the video screen. "Don't procrastinate doing this just because you want to hear it said more pret-tily by the wordsmith herself."

"I mean...it would help to know that these aren't just the sleep-deprived delusions of my brother, who is seven years sick of me mooning over Daniel."

"Fine." Jack grumbled as he got to his feet. "I'm hanging up now, but I'll message you the consensus soon. You okay with Emma chiming in as well?"

Hazel shook her head. "I mean, why not? At this point, I'll take any advice I can get. I'm this close to posting my life story on Reddit to get strangers to weigh in on my love life."

"Or lack thereof," said Jack. "I'm hanging up now. Bye."

As soon as he was gone, Hazel felt the spaciousness of the room and just how alone she was in it. She wasn't normally someone who disliked her own company, who couldn't entertain herself when no one was around. But with the unfamiliar and uncomfortable feelings coursing through her veins, it was costing her a good deal of energy to stay put where she was.

She felt like she could bolt out of the hotel and straight across the street, her bubbling feelings powerful enough to propel her right into the water. Maybe that would cool her off and—eventually—settle her down.

She stood and began to pace the room, willing Jack to respond to her. If he got caught up in one of those movies and forgot about her, or if he simply decided it was for her own good to not get a response from him, they were going to have their first real fight since the backseat wars of their childhood.

On her twelfth turn, her phone buzzed. She hurried to pick it up, her eyes landing on the most important words in the notification waiting there on her screen.

"The verdict is in, and we all say this is a good thing. Go for it, Hazel."

Before the screen even went dark, she was slipping on her shoes and flying out the door, in search of Oliver.

Eighteen

Hazel made it to the lobby before she realized she didn't even know where to find Oliver. When they had parted ways after breakfast, she had promised to text him, to make a new plan for their next hangout. But she was so caught up in the encouragement her brother, Claire, and even Emma had given her that she had run out of that room without even thinking about her next steps.

In the lobby, she turned in a slow circle, willing her intuition to send her in the right direction to find Oliver, wondering if it would be some indication of whether or not they were meant to be if she was able to do just that. As she was weighing whether to venture into the cafe or to see if her sixth sense could direct her right to his room, a movement out on the street in front of the hotel caught her eye. There, his familiar profile hunkered against the wind, was Oliver, jogging across the street towards the sea.

She flew out the door after him, calling his name, but the same wind that had him turning up his collar and the waves crashing on the shore carried her words away. Instead, she simply kept jogging, wind whipping her hair around her face, only catching up with him once he made it to the sand and was slipping off his shoes.

"Oliver," she gasped, catching her breath. "There you are."

His eyes went wide as he took in her bedraggled state. "Here I am. Were you...did you get into a fight with some pigeons to make it here? I just..." His next words tumbled out. "It's not that you don't look as beautiful as ever, but there is a certain...intensity...that suggests you may have just flown here, flapping your wings the whole way." Taking in her full appearance then, he frowned. "And where's your coat? Here, take mine."

Before she could even protest, he had slipped his jacket from his shoulders and positioned it over hers. He was wearing a crewneck sweatshirt, she was pleased to see—because she was cold, but she would have felt wrong wearing his jacket while he shivered in a t-shirt.

"I was looking for you," she said.

"I see that," he replied. "And you found me, so good job to you."

"I wanted to talk to you."

Jack nodded, then gestured to the water's edge. "Walk with me?"

Hazel slipped off her shoes and fell into step beside him, finding herself suddenly at a loss or words, unsure where to begin. She bit her lower lip and glanced at Oliver, not even trying to hide the panic that must surely be written on her face.

"Is it about Daniel?" he asked, giving her an encouraging nod. "He was really different at breakfast. A lot nicer to be around, actually. And you said...well, you said something changed between the two of you, right?" When she nodded, he gave her a small smile. "Tell me more about that."

"It's uh...well, gosh. This is kind of awkward, and I'm kind of nervous about it," she said, refusing to look at him, her eyes trained on the sand as if there might be a pressure-sensitive tripwire that it was her crucial mission to avoid. "I'll just say it. I think I stopped having feelings for Daniel because of you."

"Because of me? Did I talk you out of it somehow? Was it the jokes we made about him? Because I do feel bad about that. It isn't like me to do that, but he was just so..."

"No," she cut in. "That was all part of his whole jerk act to push me away." She shook her head. "It was misguided, but I get why he did it."

He paused for a moment. "So it worked? That's what made you stop liking him?"

"No." She turned to look at him then. "It was you, like I said."

"I...what do you mean?" He stopped then, turning to stand with his back to the sea, standing between her and the waves. "Talk to me, Hazel."

"You have treated me better than he ever did, even before he knew about my feelings. And I don't say that to put him down, because he's my best friend for a reason. I just mean...well, being with you is like a whole different experience than being with him. And I think it made me realize that there are some things that are important to me in a relationship and in a partner and that those were things I was never going to get with Daniel."

"Ah." Oliver gave her a small smile, then resumed walking along the beach. "I'm glad to hear that then. You should know that you deserve better than trying to convince someone to care about you the way you deserve to be cared about."

"That's exactly what Jack and Claire said." Hazel nodded. "My brother, remember?"

"I do. I remember everything you've told me." He gave her that small smile again. "I listen to you. I care about what you think and feel and want to share. And I guess that's why you now know that you deserve to be with someone who does the same thing."

"No, Oliver." She put her hand on his arm. "I'm just going to say it, even though it kind of scares the shit out of me. I don't just mean that you are providing me with examples to add to my list of the sort of guy I might maybe want to be with someday." She took a deep breath. "I mean that, specifically, it's you. I like *you*. A lot. I think you're the best, and I don't know what you think about that, but I just wanted you to know. And I'm sorry if it's a cliche that I just went from liking one guy to liking another one, but Jack and Claire said it wasn't the same thing and that I shouldn't try to stop liking you just because I've been hung up on Daniel for so long and that maybe this was different and that—"

"Hazel." Oliver put his hands on her upper arms, holding her in place, his eyes trained on hers, waiting for her to let him speak.

"Yes?" She blinked up at him, more frightened of what he might say next than she ever had been any time she had poured her heart out to Daniel before.

"This is different," he said. "I'm not Daniel. I like you, too. I've liked you since the beginning. I was more than happy to be your friend because, honestly, I would be anything that you would let me be." He leaned towards her then, his forehead drifting towards hers before he pulled himself back to look down into her eyes. "I think I'm rambling, too, but the fact of it is that, well, I think I feel the same way you do." He grinned at her then. "I think this could be the beginning of...well, of something."

She reached for his hands, clasping them the way she wanted to hold onto his words.

Gosh, he was so cute when he blushed. Hazel squeezed Oliver's fingers in her own, the broadest smile splitting her face. "I can't believe," she said. "Really? This is, like, totally unfamiliar territory for me. Uncharted waters, you might say. I mean...someone I like actually likes me back?" She mimed an explosion next to her head. "Mind officially blown."

"Well, it's true. Even if saying that I like you actually feels like a totally childish thing to describe what I actually feel." Oliver's pupils were dark, his tongue darting out to moisten his lips.

"What...uh...what feels like a more appropriate word, then?"

He shrugged. "I don't know. I'm not the word wizard here. But like feels too small and it's definitely too soon for love."

"Definitely," Hazel agreed, making a mental note for her heart to slow its roll. "What if we just smash those two words together to create something new that lands right in the middle of them?"

"Like...what?" Oliver frowned.

"Um...how about *loike*? It's a fun word, plus it sounds like you're saying like with a cool accent. Like Steve Irwin, sort of?"

"I *loike* you," Oliver tested it out, smiling at her and then shaking his head. "It's ridiculous, but I like it. Might even say I *loike* it."

"Me, too. And I *loike* you, too."

He was still looking at her, still smiling like he had won a contest, and Hazel's heart reminded her that this was no time to relax and stop being prone to anxious thoughts and feelings. She had spent so much of her life—the vast majority of it, in fact—hung up on Daniel that she had missed all the major milestones of most of her peers' romantic experiences. Oh, she had kissed a few frogs and been on a few dates, but finding herself in a situation like this, where there was a handsome man holding her hands and there was no reason under the sun for the two of them to not be together?

Well, that was an entirely new experience, and she worried for the first time since meeting Oliver that she might not know how to measure up. That the silences that stretched between them might become charged in a way she didn't know how to manage. Did everything change when the relationship went from a simple friendship to something much more complicated? When you added in flirtation and declarations of feelings, would they lose that old ease they had shared?

"Shall we...?" Hazel nodded to the beach stretching ahead of them, and the two of them set off walking along the coastline again, this time with Hazel's hand firmly clasped between Oliver's fingers.

They walked in silence for a time before she finally spoke. "I...I don't actually know how any of this is supposed to work. Considering that I've never had a declaration of feelings end with anything but heartbreak, um...what comes next?"

Oliver squeezed her hand. "First of all, I'd ask you very nicely to stop talking about yourself like you're the queen of being rejected romantically. While that may have been true in the past, it clearly isn't any more, and there's no reason at all to keep holding onto that identity." He looked over at her. "It's okay not to know what to do, and it doesn't mean you need to put yourself down. We're going to figure this out together."

"Oh. Okay." If there was some semblance of comfort in the knowledge that she wasn't on her own in this, it didn't do anything to dispel the unease at not knowing what happened next.

"I, uh...well, it's not like I want to know what's going to happen next year or even in a week and a half when I go back to new York and you go back to Detroit." Hazel sighed. "I'm trying to be a little better with not knowing what comes next, but it's sort of the nature of my existence, you know? As a teacher, I mean? I can't show up for class just ready to go with the flow, and I need to know what's on the plan for a week from now in case I need to prepare materials for a substitute."

"True," he replied, nodding along. "Why don't we take it a day at a time? That seems like it's generally a good pace for life, considering it's all we ever get to live in at once."

Off her expression, he shook his head at himself. "Look at me, the amateur philosopher. Apparently neither the past nor the future exist and all we have is this moment. But that's really the sort of thing an amateur philosopher says to get someone to sleep with him, and I promise that isn't what I'm trying to do."

"Right." Hazel was so grateful for the cold wind in that moment, easier to blame the redness of her cheeks on it than on the blush that was currently lighting her on fire from within. "Good to know."

Oliver groaned. "I am no good at this either, Hazel. Any ability I had to be light-hearted and charming and funny probably flew out the window the second you told me you liked me. Let's just forget I said anything about sleeping together. Put a pin in that conversation to be reexamined at a later date. Deal?"

She nodded. "Deal. But you were talking about making a plan just for today, so let's get back to that. What did you have in mind?"

"A proper date," he said without hesitation. "I know we've approximated it a few times, but we should do it for real this time."

"I agree," she said. "What should we eat? Where should we go?"

"First and most importantly, could you please wear that blue dress of yours again?" Oliver blinked at her. "You were so beautiful in it the other night, and I was working overtime to stop myself from fully appreciating it, or I would have swooned on the spot."

"Stop it," she said, pushing him a few inches further into the water. "But okay, I'll wear it. Should we go to the seafood restaurant again? The place from the first night?"

Oliver was quiet, contemplating her words. "Why not? It seems to be a night for repeating things but giving them a new flavor, so...that seems kind of perfect. We won't invite Daniel along this time, and we'll even hold hands when we walk there."

"I like the sound of that."

And then, just as she had feared they would no longer be able to do, the two of them lapsed into comfortable silence, their hands anchoring them together as they walked the beach, the cold water kissing their ankles. The smiles on their faces matched each other, and they took turns darting glances at the other and squeezing their hands.

When they reached the point to turn around, Oliver lifted Hazel's hand to his mouth, pressing a soft kiss across the back of her knuckles. "Thank you," he said as they began walking again.

"For what? I'm not exactly doing charity here," she said, a chuckle in her voice.

"For coming here. For being you. For being brave today and initiating this conversation. For not getting scared of the unknown, but staying right here by my side."

At his mention of the unknown, Hazel felt a shiver up her spine. Without even knowing it, he had hit the nail right on the head of one of her bigger fears. What if she woke up in the morning so scared by the unfamiliar and the idea of intimacy and vulnerability that she somehow undid it all? What if she ran away, or at least ran back to the familiarity of Daniel and unrequited love?

"I'm doing the best I can," she said, "but I can't promise I'll always be brave. I'm a giant wimp in my heart of hearts."

Oliver shook his head resolutely. "I don't believe that for even a second. And that's what I'm here for, anytime you need me. We're going to figure this out together."

Nineteen

Hazel was getting ready for her date in the room when Daniel came back, looking flustered and happy as he gave her a big smile and sank onto his bed.

"Good day?" she asked over her shoulder. She was styling her hair in the mirror, already wearing her dress and just trying to capture the perfect messy waves she had managed her previous time wearing it.

"It was great," Daniel breathed. "So much more fun to spend the day with, you know, *people*, instead of on my own seeing how fast I can walk up a hill. Not that I didn't love the ruins I got to see," he hurried to add. "I think it's all about striking the right balance. Zoe is pretty tiring too, in her own way. I guess 7-year-olds don't take naps anymore, do they? They just keep going and going until the adults are the ones who get overtired and slink off to a dark room somewhere."

She had to laugh at that. "Welcome to my world, Daniel. I wish at least once a week that my third graders still took naps, but then again, I might be the world's biggest proponent of napping. I tried to convince Oliver to take a nap the other day, but I guess I'm not as much of a nap apologist as I'd like to be because it definitely didn't work."

Daniel smiled, lifting his head to look at her. "Um, you look nice. Going somewhere? You have a date or something?"

When she nodded, his jaw dropped. "Are you kidding me? Dang, Haze, you move fast, don't you?" She must have looked stricken because he continued. "No, I'm just teasing. This is a long time coming. If you hadn't been hung up on me, you would have been snapped up by some lucky guy years ago."

"Ew, Daniel," she chided. "I am not something to be snapped up. But you are definitely right that it's time to start spending time with adult men who are interested in me the same way I'm interested in them."

He nodded, a broad smile on his face. "Absolutely. So you're going out with Oliver, then? Like, on a proper date?"

She frowned. "How did you know that?"

Daniel rolled his eyes. "Oh, please. You've been spending every day with him, and you're practically dating him already. Who else would it be? Mr. Schuler? I don't think Mrs. Schuler would approve of that."

"You're ridiculous." She glanced at him in the mirror. "So it isn't weird for you that I'm dating your coworker? I didn't even consider until just this moment that maybe I should have talked it over with you first."

"Why?" He wrinkled his nose. "It's your life, Hazel, and you should do what makes you happy. Spend it with whoever you want to spend it with. The only way I'd have a problem with that is if you were spending it with someone who didn't deserve you."

"Right." She nodded. "And that's not the case here because Oliver is actually a really good guy and you were just pretending to have beef with him because you got the idea in your head that you had to alienate everyone within a ten-foot radius of you."

"Something like that. Have no fear though, I've seen the error of my ways, and Good Daniel is here to stay." He smiled. "And you're right about Oliver. He's the best. Now that I think about it, the two of you are actually a really great match, and I don't know why I didn't think of it before."

"Hmm." Hazel tapped on her lower lip and gave an exaggerated look up at the ceiling. "Can't begin to guess why you weren't trying to set me up with eligible bachelors. It's not like I gave you any reason to think I wouldn't be interested in that."

He laughed just once as he pushed himself to his feet. "I'm going to head out."

"Again?" She turned to look at him. "Look at you, Mr. Social. What are you up to now?"

Daniel wouldn't quite make eye contact with her, his hand coming up to rub the back of his neck. "Well, actually, Elliot and Anya asked me to do them a little favor. I guess Zoe has a play date with Mr. Schuler's grandkids, and they wanted a little time to themselves."

"Oh, right." She paused a moment, taking in his nervous demeanor. "So...you and Nora will be the ones supervising this play date, then?"

Daniel nodded, still finding anywhere else to look but right at her. Hazel sighed. She couldn't blame him for not wanting to confide in her that he was spending time with a woman, not after the way she had carried that torch for him like it was a line on her resume.

"I'm glad you're spending time with her," she said, earning her a surprised glance. "All of them really, but especially Nora. She's not having an easy time of it, is she? I feel so bad for her, and for the kids, too."

"How did you...?" Daniel's face was the picture of confusion.

"Oliver and I sat with her for a bit the other night, and she told us about her late husband. If you can bring a little joy into her day, I hope you do." She held up a hand. "I'm not asking you to cure her of her grief. That's not even a thing. But if you can, I don't know, get her attention out of that cavern of grief and direct it somewhere else for a bit. I'm sure she'll appreciate it."

"I'll bring my A game," said Daniel, a smile that had a self-consciousness to it spreading on his face. "Better grab a coffee, though, or else it'll be my Z game. Get it? Because I would be sleeping." He sighed. "That's really the kind of joke that would work better if I were a comic strip character, isn't it?"

Hazel chuckled and shook her head. "Get out of here. I'm sure they're waiting for you, and your jokes would absolutely kill with the 8-year-old crowd. They're wasted on me."

She was still smiling when he left, a lightness in her chest as she took in her appearance in the mirror. With just a dab of tinted lip gloss, she was ready to head out and meet

Oliver for their first official date, and all was right in her world.

The two evenings that Hazel had spent at the seafood restaurant down the road couldn't have been more different. At the first outing, she had felt like one of the guys, just tagging along as she watched the two men on either side of her lob jokes and pointed comments, unsure of what any of it meant or, at times, what she was even doing there.

Tonight, though, she had had the undivided attention of Oliver from the first moment their eyes had met, walked on his arm to the restaurant, and even sat next to him again, both of them taking the prime view of the sea and sharing it.

The only constant was the food, but Hazel was sure that even that was better this time around. Without the anxiety of what Daniel's snide comments and attitude adjustment could mean, and without the unwanted burden of unrequited love weighing her down, all the flavors were amplified. The lemon was sharper, the butter was richer, the umami of the fish was more mouthwateringly delicious than Hazel could remember.

From the beginning to the end, it was precisely the kind of date she would have written for herself, if she could have scripted it into existence. She told Oliver just that as they arrived back at the hotel.

"Wow, really? I didn't miss any of the key components of a perfect date in your book?"

She tilted her head to the side. "Oh, I don't know. If we could have added in a carnival with some scary rides and you winning me a giant teddy bear, that might have pushed it right over the edge into perfection territory."

"Good to know. I know what I'll be looking up online when I get back to my room."

Hazel put her hand on his forearm. "Please, don't. That may have been a bluff on my part. Unless you want to find out just how sensitive my stomach is, I highly suggest we don't go on any rides, at least not within hours of even thinking about eating."

"I promise not to take you on any roller coasters on our next date," he said, putting his free hand over his heart before turning to her. "That reminds me, though...looks like our next date is going to be Christmas Eve, assuming you want to spend tomorrow with me as well. Is that okay? I know there's the whole company Christmas party thing, and if you don't feel comfortable being, well, a couple there, then that's okay. You can just go as Daniel's friend and we can keep it all under the radar. It might even be kind of fun that way, you know? The thrill of the secret?" He pulled a face. "Can you tell I've never had a secret workplace romance?"

"I can, and I think I *loike* it," she said, standing on her toes to drop a kiss on his cheek. "But I don't think there's anything wrong with us going together. The main people we will probably spend time with there have already seen us together, and it's not like it's the scandal of the century that Daniel's friend ended up becoming Oliver's girlfriend." Her face flushed with heat as she realized what she had said. "I mean Oliver's date. But also that, you know, it's not like Daniel and I were married or even dating." She laughed then. "And it's not like anyone who mistakenly thought we were was able to live in that delusion for long, judging by the way Jerk Daniel so quickly corrected them and introduced me with a nickname that made them all question my sanity." She sniffed out a laugh. "No, I think it's just fine for us to show up as a couple. The people who know us will be happy for us, and for the people who don't know us, maybe we'll provide a little bit of entertainment for them."

"That's a good way of looking at it," said Oliver, pausing as the hotel's automatic door opened to let them in. "And good save with that whole 'girlfriend' bit." He gave her the sort of smile that let her know he had enjoyed every moment of her discomfort about that particular slip up. "I agree that it's too soon to talk about things like that, but I'm hopeful that we can get a conversation on the agenda by the end of our stay in Turkey."

Hazel's eyes widened, surprised at just how soon Oliver expected to be comfortable talking about their relationship in terms of where it was going. "Good to know," she said with a nod. "Have your secretary call my secretary and we'll find a time that works for both of us."

"Indeed."

Now that they were in from the cold, Hazel let her hand drop away from the crook of Oliver's arm, no longer needing his warmth. As her hand slipped back to her side, he caught it in his own, walking her hand in hand all the way to her room. She wondered for a moment if Daniel was inside, if he was listening from the other side and rooting them on. Briefly, she hoped that he might still be keeping

Nora company, that the unexpected pairing of the two of them might be creating a unique kind of magic of their own.

"Thank you for a perfect night," said Hazel, leaning back against the door and just hoping that, if Daniel was inside, at least he wouldn't open the door.

"Even without the carnival rides and giant teddy bear," replied Oliver, hanging his head.

She reached for his chin and pulled it forward, bringing his eyes back up to meet hers. "It was perfect." And then, because she had waited long enough for something to happen the way she had wanted it to, and because she had been brave that day and confessed her feelings, and because every moment that she had spent with Oliver that evening had felt like heaven and peace and thrill all rolled up into one...

Because of all of that, she pushed herself up on her toes and pulled Oliver closer, his mouth coming down to find hers.

When their lips met, she couldn't stop a sigh from escaping her lips. He was warm and firm and he tasted like the coffee they had sipped after dinner and the vanilla ice cream they had shared and the clove pods that had been waiting in a dish when he had paid the check. When he had asked the server about them, she had said they were for fresh breath after eating that much fish, and both Hazel and Oliver had slipped one between their teeth as they had walked back to the hotel.

If Hazel had known just how intoxicating the taste of a clove would be on Oliver's lips, she would have slipped the whole dish in her bag. Of course, it might not be the cloves that were so intoxicating after all.

Oliver pulled back, his pupils blown as his eyes tracked her face and the flush that had surely risen on her cheeks.

"You are beautiful," he said. "And I will miss you terribly until I see you again in the morning." He pressed one more gentle, chaste kiss on her lips, squeezed her hand, and stepped back, waiting for her to unlock her door and step inside before he set off down the hallway to his own room.

Inside, Hazel leaned back against the door, her hand coming up to touch her lips, feeling the faintest reminder of Oliver there.

Only then, as she was reminiscing about a kiss that had simultaneously felt like coming home and setting off on a marvelous adventure, as she was letting herself relive the moment while it was still this fresh in her mind, did she look up to find Daniel's bed mercifully empty.

"Oh, thank goodness," she breathed, slipping off her shoes and reaching to unzip her dress. "We may have gotten out of the tricky crush territory, but we are *not* ready for the girl talk phase of our friendship yet."

Twenty

There were two more special dresses in Hazel's suitcase, one each saved for Christmas and New Year's. When she had packed, she hadn't considered just how often she would want to be in her fanciest attire, or just how many occasions there would be to put on her finery and strut around with a handsome man on her arm.

Or with her on his arm. However that worked.

It was early the following evening, Christmas Eve, and she was weighing her options for the party the Schuler Group was hosting in the hotel restaurant.

At breakfast that morning, Hazel had been surprised to see it was business as usual everywhere. She asked one of the servers, a familiar young woman named Beyza who was frequently manning the coffee station, if everyone was still working, even though it was Christmas.

Beyza had given her a puzzled look, then said that yes, when it was Christmas in a week, some of them would have the day off.

"But it's Christmas Eve *today*," Hazel had said, "and Christmas Day is tomorrow. Are you talking about New Year's Eve?"

Beyza nodded. "Yes, December 31st. I already have my New Year's gifts ready and my Santa hat to wear. I'll be working that day, but I will dress up with all of you."

When Hazel had returned to the table and shared the encounter with Oliver and everyone else there, she had been greeted by a number of confused expressions. Only Daniel seemed unfazed by it. "Well, it isn't a Christian country, so it makes sense that they would celebrate on December 31st. It is all a bit confusing, though."

"Right, and what about the Santa hats?" Hazel asked. "That was particularly puzzling to me."

"Oh, I know this one!" crowed Oliver, looking pleased with himself. "We're actually quite close to the birthplace of St. Nicholas. There's a city nearby, Demre, I think it's called, with a museum there and everything." He looked at Zoe with excitement in his eyes. "Maybe we should see if we can arrange a little excursion there in the next few days? After Santa has time to finish delivering all the presents, of course."

Zoe rolled her eyes. "I already know that Santa isn't real, Oliver. Besides, even if he were, it sounds like people here would expect him to deliver their presents on New Year's Eve, so it's not like he would be finished working after tonight." She tucked her hands in her lap, sitting up a little straighter. "I do enjoy a good trip to the museum though, so if my parents are up for it, that would be nice. Maybe Mr. Schuler's grandkids can come too."

Daniel coughed, pounding on his chest like he was trying to dislodge something there, at the mention of Mr. Schuler's family.

Hazel leaned towards him. "Oh, that's right. I never asked you how your play date went." She wiggled her eyebrows at him, and he elbowed her away, back towards Oliver. "Okay, okay," she said, raising her hands. "I can take a hint." Dropping her voice to a stage whisper, she added, "We'll talk later, then."

But now it was almost time for the Christmas party, and Hazel still hadn't decided which dress to wear. Daniel had already left, seeming to avoid being alone with her after her earlier teasing about Nora. She took each dress from the wardrobe where she had hung them, one that was emerald green and one that was black with silver details on it.

Suddenly, they both felt entirely too dressy, and she was self conscious just imagining having to walk out to the lobby by herself. What if everyone else was taking things a little more casually this evening? What if she had missed the dress code for this party entirely? What if Oliver took one look at her, glanced down at his business casual attire, and then changed his mind, realizing that she was actually too much work to be worth it?

Part of her knew she was being ridiculous, but that didn't change the feeling. She flailed, not sure what to do next. She had already video called her family back home, wishing them a happy day and showing them the view from her hotel room. If she called back now with some kind of wardrobe crisis, that just might be enough to undo all the effort she had put into showing them she was an adult who had her act together.

Jack and Claire had even taken the phone into the other room to hear all about her date with Oliver, and judging by the smiles on her parents faces, they were nearly as well informed as the younger generation was about all the latest happenings in Hazel's love life and at least equally pleased.

While she was still pondering her next steps, her phone vibrated with a new message from Oliver.

"I'm about ready to head to the lobby. You?"

She grimaced, her fingers already firing off her reply before she could second guess it.

"No, not really. I'm having a crisis of confidence and can't decide what to wear. Do you want to come here and give me an unbiased opinion?"

His response came almost as quickly as hers had.

"There won't be anything unbiased about it, but I'm happy to come tell you how beautiful you look. Be there in five."

Hazel smiled to herself, already feeling her anxiety leeching from her stomach, replaced by a similar and yet significantly different fluttering feeling. These were nerves, but they were excited ones. There was nothing scary about them.

She opened the door a moment later when Oliver knocked, escorting him inside and then immediately holding up both of the dresses as he took a seat on the end of Daniel's bed. His gaze tracked from one dress to the other, ultimately settling on Hazel's smile.

"They both look gorgeous," he said. "And you will look beautiful in either one."

"They aren't...I don't know...too much?" she asked, chewing her lower lip for a second before remembering she had already put on her red lipstick. She leaned over to check the mirror, making sure she hadn't gotten lipstick on her teeth. "You walked through the lobby to come here, and there must have been some other women there already. What were they wearing? Is this dress going to fit in there?"

"I..." Oliver suddenly looked every bit the clueless man, the type who wouldn't know if an event was legging appropriate or if it was acceptable to wear white to a wedding.

"You weren't paying attention," she said, her heart sinking. She took him in then, his tailored black suit and a bow tie that looked like he had tied it himself. "What about the men? Were they dressed like you?"

Oliver nodded. "It's definitely a formal event, Haze. I didn't see any khakis or untucked shirts. And I'm sure the women are dressed up." He nodded to the two dresses. "Whichever one you choose, you'll be perfect. And the other one will be great for the next party. The New Year's Eve one."

Hazel pursed her lips in thought. "I'll go with the green then. Leave the black one—it's a little sexier," she added, touching the side to reveal a high slit that made Oliver's eyes go impossibly wide. "And green is festive." She nodded then, decision made. "Okay, then. I'll go change."

Oliver got to his feet. "Er...should I go?" He gestured to the door. "I can meet you in the lobby, like we planned."

"No need." She shook her head. "I'll just pop into the bathroom, change, and then we can walk together. Won't be a minute."

When she reemerged from the bathroom, her hair falling around her shoulders and the green dress that so perfectly brought out the golden undertones in it, Oliver was silent, his jaw agape.

"You look..." He swallowed. "Yeah, you look amazing." He got to his feet, offering his arm. "Shall we?"

The hotel had prepared a special Christmas Eve feast for the Schuler Group employees and their guests, complete with roast turkeys, mashed potatoes, stuffing, and homemade gravy. It was all so delicious—and so reminiscent of the recent Thanksgiving she had spent with her family—that Hazel immediately settled in to the familial warmth of it all.

There had been a cocktail hour at the beginning, where they had circulated, catching up with the people they had spent the most time with over the last few days and sharing greetings with a few new friends as well. Hazel was tickled to see Daniel deep in conversation with Nora, the two of them watching as her children and Zoe sat rapt, listening to Mr. Schuler read them a Christmas book.

Any concerns she may have had about being overdressed had flown out the window as soon as she had seen Mrs. Schuler, the elderly woman wearing a tiara that perfectly complimented the ruby red high-necked gown she was wearing. "You look beautiful," Hazel had whispered to her as they exchanged greetings.

"As do you, my dear," Mrs. Schuler had replied, wiggling her eyebrows in the direction of Oliver. "The two of you make a very handsome couple."

"I knew it!" a voice sounded from behind them, and they turned to find Elliot, Austin, and their respective spouses milling about behind them. "We had a little bet going about the two of you," Anya continued. "All in good fun, of course. But after sharing a few meals with you both, even the most oblivious of us"—here she shot a glare at her husband—"could see that there was something there. Glad to see the two of you seem to have figured it out."

Hazel felt the firm pressure of Oliver's hand on her lower back a moment before he wrapped his arm around her waist, pulling her to his side. "Thank you," he said. "I'm pretty pleased that it didn't take us too long to figure it out, but I have to give Hazel all the credit for being the one to speak up first. If I had been left to my own devices, I might be eating Christmas dinner alone, mooning over her from afar without even realizing that I had feelings for her yet."

"You sound like me," said Elliot.

Anya was already nodding. "Don't even ask how long I had to drop hints before this one asked me out. We might still be doing that dance if it hadn't been for that one party."

"That's right. A President's Day party the university put on, if I remember correctly."

"Indeed," said Anya. "Never underestimate the magic of the holidays. Even the ones that don't seem particularly romantic can sometimes help spur things in the right direction. You two are lucky that you got together at Christmas, though. It's the best of the romantic holidays." She dropped her voice. "Don't tell Valentine's Day that I said that. And don't tell my daughter that I said Christmas is a romantic holiday, or she's likely to stage yet another protest."

"A protest?" Hazel asked, chuckling. "I have to say, even as someone who spends most of her days with other kids her age, she never ceases to amaze."

"Oh yes, a protest, and not her first," piped up Elliot. "I believe the latest one was motivated by animal rights. Specifically, our cat's right to wear matching outfits with Zoe."

Hazel was still laughing at Zoe's antics when she felt Oliver steering her towards a nearby high top table, where he offered her a glass of champagne.

She accepted the glass, raising it to clink against his. "Hi," she said, when she found his eyes on hers. "Having fun?"

"Oh, absolutely." He nodded. "I suspect even the profit-and-loss meeting we're having in a few days would be fun if I had you there with me."

"I'm more than happy to join," she replied. "Don't exactly have a packed social calendar for the next week."

"No, I guess you don't. Or rather, you didn't. It's quite full now that you're spending all your time with me."

Hazel murmured her agreement, then took another sip of her champagne, looking at the Christmas lights that were glowing outside the window. "It's hard not to wonder what will happen next," she blurted. "I know I should just enjoy being in the moment, but when everyone is telling us that we're such a lovely couple, so lucky to have found each other..." She let out a sigh. "It's almost impossible for me not to wonder what's going to happen when this is over."

Concern crowded Oliver's features. "When this is over?"

"This trip, I mean." She shook her head. "I'm not thinking about *us* being over. Believe it or not, I'm trying not to think things that will depress me and make me ruin my makeup. I'm also not thinking about sad dog and cat stories I've stumbled onto on the internet that still haunt me to this day."

Oliver nodded. "Those are the worst. You're just scrolling along, watching a nice video and suddenly someone is telling you the most heartbreaking story of a cat that got abandoned by its owner or something, and then they just expect you to go on with your day." He gazed off into the distance for a second, then shook his head as if coming back to himself. "But that's not the biggest concern, not right now." He reached over for her hand, clasping it on top of the table. "I don't want to think about this being over, either. And that's why I think we're going to have to talk, maybe sooner than we had planned, about what this relationship actually is and what we're willing to do to make it work."

"But that's..." Hazel shook her head. "Isn't that a crazy thing to even think about with someone you met a week ago that you still barely even know?"

"When you put it like that, then...yeah. At face value, it's a completely bizarre concept, calling someone your girlfriend or boyfriend within a week of even learning that they exist. It's also crazy to think about making that relationship long distance or one of you relocating to a new part of the country after that short of a time. If my 13-year-old sister said the things to me that I'm thinking about doing for you, I would want to physically restrain her to keep her from throwing her life away for a 13-year-old-boy."

"Yeah." Hazel nodded her head earnestly at him. "That's pretty much how I feel. Apart from the whole thing with Daniel, I pretty much pride myself on being levelheaded. Not doing impulsive things. In fact, the whole Daniel thing was probably part of that, because what is more rational and the opposite of impulsive than consistently holding onto feelings for someone who absolutely, positively, will not reciprocate them?"

"Okay, but..." Oliver pulled his lower lip into his mouth, studying her. "But why does it feel different when it's you and me than it does when it's my hypothetical teenage sister and her hypothetical teenage boyfriend?"

Hazel wrinkled her nose. "Because we aren't hormonal teenagers?"

"Yeah, I guess that's a big part of it." Oliver nodded. "We've proven our abilities to, well, survive as adults in the world. So that makes thinking things like this romantic rather than bone-headed." He shrugged. "I don't exactly know what to tell you. I know I love being with you, and I strongly suspect I'm going to want to keep being with you even after we're back in the US and hundreds of miles apart. But that doesn't mean I have a magical solution tucked up my sleeve that is going to make all this make sense."

Hazel huffed out a humorless laugh. "You mean you don't conveniently have plans to transfer to the Schuler Group's New York office in the next few months? Because it would be awfully convenient if you did, and now would be a great time to share it."

He shook his head, a sadness creasing his forehead and making her want to smooth the lines away. "I don't. Not right now, anyway. And, as much as I want to know where this thing between us is going to go, I don't think making an impulsive cross-country move right now is the thing to do."

"It isn't," she agreed. Hazel was relieved when he stepped closer, putting his arm around her and just gazing out at the water with her. She let herself lean against his shoulder, trying to force away the thoughts that were threatening to steal her happiness away.

It was a losing battle.

Twenty-One

The days passed in a blur, highlighted by the time Hazel spent with Oliver, the moments they shared talking over beers, reading silently together, walking more steps every day than she did in an entire weekend back home.

As much as she looked forward to his company, as much as she jumped out of bed in the morning eager to see him, her sadness and anxiety at being parted soon followed her around like a dark cloud that was tethered to her on a very short leash. Hazel reminded herself at regular intervals to try to live in the moment, to try to enjoy the time she had because tomorrow wasn't a guarantee...and yet, more often than not, she found herself worried about tomorrow and what it would look like.

How would Oliver fit into it? Was it even possible to keep him in her life, or were they just prolonging the inevitable? Would it ultimately have been less painful if she had never even met him? Knowing him now, and especially knowing the joy of being a special person in his life, and then having that stripped away was bound to be more painful than any rejection she had ever experienced at Daniel's hands.

She took some joy, at least, in the fact that Daniel seemed to be flourishing. No longer was he spending his days treating himself like some kind of beast mode hyperproductivity experiment. Instead, he was spending the days, by all her observations, at least, soaking up all that Antalya had to offer. He was often found joining Elliot and family on an excursion, or doing the same with Mr. Schuler's family. If Hazel had still been holding onto her old feelings for Daniel, all of this family time would probably be adding an extra layer of yearning, making her wish not only that they could be together but that they could have a family of their own.

As it was, there had been no regression, no morning after questioning, no doubts at all about trading in her unrequited yearning for the mutual admiration of her relationship with Oliver.

"No, but at least that was a familiar kind of pain," she murmured to herself as she sorted through the clothes she wanted to send to the hotel's laundry service. "This new kind and the uncertainty of all of it just might be the thing that finally breaks my heart in two."

In the foul mood that she was in, Hazel sent Oliver a quick message to let him know that she needed the morning to herself. Her anxieties about the future had been their constant companions the last few days, despite all her best efforts to keep them tucked neatly away where they couldn't ruin a perfectly good day. Still, it was New Year's Eve, and it was bound to be a late night full of big conversations about the future. As much as she was looking forward to hearing all of her new friends' big plans for the next year, she knew she wouldn't enjoy the inevitable questions she and Oliver would get. The best thing for it was to take at least the morning for herself, to try every trick in her arsenal to convince herself to be in a happy, "seize the moment" sort of mental space.

After Oliver replied to let her know he'd be available whenever she wanted to spend time together, she set off on her own to walk the beach, tossing on a scarf against the chilly breeze that was in the air.

She walked until her ears started to hurt from the cold air blowing over them, and even then she just hiked up her scarf a little higher and kept going. She kept waiting for the moment where she would feel peace or where she would have some deeper understanding of how it was all going to work, but it just didn't happen.

And so she kept walking.

When she found herself so far down the beach that she couldn't make out which of the hotels dotting the road belonged to her, she resolved to go just a little further—"just five more minutes"—and then begin to make her way back. If something transformational didn't happen in those next few moments, then it was unlikely to come before she needed to face the evening celebration and all its inevitable future talk.

On her way back, when Hazel had finally moved on from wracking her brain for an easy solution that would keep her and Oliver together—he had already made it clear he wasn't secretly planning a move to New York, and she couldn't even consider moving without knowing more about how her teacher certification would cross state lines—she started to ask why. Why had she and Oliver even found each other if it wasn't going to be a source of long-term happiness for them? What was even the point?

Maybe this was all just about getting you to realize that it was time to move on. To see what was out there. Maybe now, when you meet the guy who is the right guy, you'll be ready for him, rather than still hung up on Daniel.

Hazel stopped in her tracks. Whatever voice in the back of her mind had offered that particular batch of wisdom, it could excuse itself right back to the pits of hell from whence it had come. "Just about getting me to move on?" she practically shouted the words at the sea. "Is that really what someone as wonderful as Oliver deserves to be reduced to? Just a plot point in my story, rather than a central character?"

She shook her head. She knew enough about romance books from reading them, and had a little bit of insight into writing them now after getting a courtside seat to Claire's process, and she knew—she *knew* it, had never been so sure of anything—that Claire would never write a character as dynamic and layered and loveable as Oliver only to have him exit stage left so that the real leading man could make his entrance.

She wanted to shake her fist at the sea, curse at the heavens, argue with the universe until she forced it to conform to her will. And yet, despite the ruins she had visited in the last weeks and all the Greek gods that had left an imprint on her subconscious mind as a result, she knew that wasn't going to accomplish anything. Poseidon didn't have a hand in her destiny. There was, simply, nothing else for her to do. She had said her piece, had searched her heart, and all that was left was to put on a pretty dress, drink some more champagne, and ring in the new year. The day after tomorrow, she would be heading home, anyway, and all of this would be over.

The black dress that Hazel had saved for New Year's Eve was waiting for her in the room when she got back to the hotel. Despite her original intention to only spend the morning wandering and getting her head on straight, it had turned into a full-day affair. She had left her phone behind, intending to focus on clearing her head rather than getting distracted by any desire to snap the perfect picture or come up with the perfect social media caption.

The texts she had missed from Oliver had increased in their concern as the hours had lapsed.

"Are you back? I'm getting hungry, might go to the cafe for a quick lunch."

"Is everything okay? Haven't heard anything from you in a while, and I'm getting a little worried."

"Hazel, should I come looking for you? Shit, I'm realizing now you might not have your phone with you. I'm going to look for you."

Reading his last message, she frowned. She hadn't seen Oliver on the beach, and so she wondered if he had simply talked himself out of it.

There wasn't much time left before they were due to meet for the party, so she sent him a quick response, letting him know that she was back, that she was okay and was sorry he had worried, and that she would be ready in twenty minutes.

"Now to do something about this hair..." As she took in her windblown appearance, she silently berated her earlier self for not at least sweeping her wavy locks up into a clip before braving the wind. She had her work cut out for her, turning her frizz into something that looked like it belonged with the dress she was about to don.

She switched on one of her favorite pump-up pop playlists on her phone, then set to work detangling her hair, sweeping it into an updo, perfecting her eyeliner, and tracing her lips with her favorite bold lipstick before slipping into the dress.

"Pretty good," she said, turning to look at her reflection over her shoulder. She forced a smile at the sad girl that was looking back at her. "Maybe it doesn't have to be so serious. Maybe you can just have a nice evening and not always be so freaking pathetic about the future."

She practically spat the words at her reflection, and she was surprised when, just a second later, there was a knock on the door. Hazel jolted before waddling over—she hadn't put her shoes on yet, and the hemline of the dress was long without her heels to boost her—checking the peephole before opening it.

Oliver was standing there, looking like something out of the third act of a 90s rom com. He should have been standing in the pouring rain, his eyes downcast, a perfect little pout on his lips, and a British accent for good measure. None of the details were right, but the demeanor was spot on. Hazel flung open the door, concern swirling around her as she reached for him, pulling him inside.

"Are you okay? What is it? You looked so sad standing there. Did something happen? Is everything okay?" She took his face in her hands, her eyes traveling his whole face, looking for some sign of what had hurt him, of who might deserve her vengeance.

Oliver forced a smile as his hands came up to her wrists, gently pulling her hands off his face. "I'm okay," he said. "Just a bit of an emotional mess, but that's nothing new these days."

His grandmother. At once, Hazel thought of the fresh grief Oliver had shared with her, of the beloved grandmother he had lost and who he didn't know how to exist in a world without, and she felt the guilt in her lower belly like a knife. All this time, she had been so focused on her anticipatory grief over not seeing Oliver every day, while he was the one being brave, the one being constant and reassuring her that everything would be okay...and at the same time, he was feeling *actual* grief for someone he had loved deeply.

"I'm so sorry, Oliver." She wrapped her arms around him, wishing she were big enough to surround him completely and protect him from the world. "It must be so hard, missing your grandma at a time like this. Going into the new year without her. Having a new person in your life and not getting to introduce her to her." That last one had hurt her, too. For as much as she *loiked*—no, scratch that, she could say that she loved him—Oliver, both his loss of not getting to introduce her to his grandma and Hazel's loss of not getting to meet one of the people most directly responsible for the kind and compassionate man that Oliver had turned out to be...well, it hurt. And if it hurt her, it must be hurting him a whole lot more.

He pulled back to look at her, his face falling as their eyes met. "Oh my god, I wasn't even thinking of that." He closed his eyes. "And now that I am, it's even worse." He leaned forward, burying his head in her hair, inhaling her deeply. "I was just worried about you, missing you, and then it hit me that I'm going to be missing you and not knowing where you are, like, all the time soon. I went to go look for you, and then I saw you way off in the distance, and I knew it wasn't going to be like that, not in a few days. I won't be able to go look for you, to retrace your steps, to see you from a distance, to touch you and reassure myself that you're okay." Oliver sighed heavily. "And you're right, it's about my grandma, too, and I didn't even realize it."

He forced himself away from her, sitting down heavily as if the bed where he perched was doing the real heavy lifting. "When you lose someone suddenly like that, it's almost impossible not to fear the same thing happening again, you know? She...she was just sleeping. And then she wasn't. She was gone. I didn't get to say goodbye to her or to know that the last day I saw her was going to be the last day that I saw her." His eyes had grown shiny with unshed tears. "And now, with you...it's like we're counting down towards this day that is going to be the last day that I see you, and I just don't know if I can handle it. I don't know if I'm strong enough to do it."

Hazel sat down next to him, reaching for his hand. "I'm struggling with it, too," she said. "But you already knew that. I haven't exactly been good at keeping my big feelings to myself."

He raised her hand, pressing it against his cheek. "And I love that about you. I don't want you to keep them to yourself. I like knowing what you're feeling, and I like helping you with it, too." His eyes were boring deep into hers. "But are we crazy to think we can do this? Is there even a future for us beyond tomorrow?"

"I..." Hazel shook her head. "I honestly don't know. It's like...I walked an entire beach today, Oliver. I practically walked to Greece, if that's even possible." She sighed. "I feel like I've always believed that if I think hard enough about a problem, I'm going to find a solution. It's like...my brain has gotten me where I am, to all the things that are good in my life, and if a solution exists to a problem that's troubling me, then it's going to come up with it."

"And did it?" Oliver asked the question like he already knew what her answer was going to be.

Hazel shook her head, sadness washing over her and threatening to ruin her perfect eyeliner. "It didn't. It told me some things that pissed me off, tried to make me feel better with some ridiculous platitudes...but no solution." She squeezed Oliver's hand then. "It doesn't mean there isn't one, I guess. Maybe it's like a Magic 8 ball, and this was more of an 'ask again later' situation."

Oliver sighed. "I hate this. I like you so much...no, I *loike* you so much..." He cursed under his breath. "I think I love you. I'm so grateful to have even met you. And I just don't want to let you go. I don't want to accept defeat like this. I don't want to let the unknown future keep us from becoming what we could be."

"I know, and I agree with all of it." She leaned her head on his shoulder. "Especially the love part. But I don't know if love is going to give us a solution to this, either. Don't they always say that love isn't enough?"

He hummed a non-verbal response. "They do, but they say a lot of other stupid shit too, so…"

Hazel let out a small laugh, bursting from her lips perfunctorily. "I think we have to accept, for now at least, that we can't know the answer. Do you think we can still find a way to enjoy the night?" As a thought occurred to her, she turned to him, trying to impart the depth of her sincerity with a deep gaze. "If it's all too much, I understand. I'd be more than happy to change back into my comfy clothes and just wallow in bed. You could go to the party without me, or you could go do the same thing in your own room. And if you don't want to see me tomorrow either, if you just want to let this lie as it is now, I'll understand that."

Oliver let out a long deep breath and Hazel felt herself deflating right along with his lungs. She had meant every word, and yet she had hoped with every one that he would interrupt her, kiss her, tell her he didn't want any of that, tell her that nothing and no one was going to keep them apart.

But instead he sighed.

Finally, he spoke, the smile he gave her small and forced. "We should still go, Hazel. We should still spend time together while we can, even if it hurts." He got to his feet, pulling on her hand. "Come on. Come with me."

Twenty-Two

*I*t *should be a crime to be this sad in a dress this pretty,* thought Hazel as she pasted on a smile, nodding at Nora as she passed by with her two children in tow.

Nora, of course, was the last person she wanted to realize she was this distraught. How embarrassing would it be to tell a recently widowed woman that you were sad because your boyfriend lived in a different state? If Nora didn't roll her eyes, Hazel would do it for her, manually, if need be.

"Where's your guy?" Nora asked, stepping up to Hazel's standing table as she shooed her kids in the direction of their grandfather. She craned her neck as she looked around for Oliver. "I've been trying to catch the two of you together for the whole evening, but it seems like he has made himself scarce." She narrowed her eyes at Hazel. "Something going on?"

Hazel shook her head as she huffed out a watery laugh, camouflaging it with a cough. "Not at all. I think he's getting us drinks. Some appetizers, maybe."

"Good." Nora nodded. "They're delicious." She put her hand on Hazel's arm, fixing her eyes intently on Hazel's as if she saw right through exactly what she was trying to hide but was—mercifully—too kind to put her on the spot. "I'll catch you both again later, then. Have a nice night, Hazel."

"You too, Nora."

Hazel waited until she was alone again to let her smile slip. It was hard work, pretending nothing was wrong when it felt like just maybe everything was. When her phone buzzed in her purse, she pulled it out, glad for the distraction.

In the group chat she shared with Jack and Claire, there was a new message from her brother. She smiled to see his name there, her big brother once again checking in on her right when she needed him. As if he hadn't already been her most reliable playmate and protector throughout their entire childhood, he somehow managed to maintain that role even well into adult life.

"You're much closer to the new year than we are here. How's the future looking?"

Hazel chuckled, already replying.

"It seems pretty much the same as the past. No flying cars, at least."

And then, because she could never bring herself to pretend with Jack, and not with Claire either, she kept writing.

"A little heartbroken, to be honest. Oliver and I are saying goodbye the day after tomorrow, and neither of us can see a path forward to making it work."

That got her a response from Claire.

"Oh, honey. I'm so sorry. But just because you haven't figured it out yet doesn't mean you won't ever figure it out, right? I mean, look at Emma. She lives in Ireland now, and Connor was considering moving to New York, if that was what it took for them to be together. You don't have to know all the answers now, you just have to keep moving in the right direction."

Hazel's eyes were wet, the words blurring on the screen as she shook her head.

"I know what you mean, but it doesn't feel that way for some reason, Claire. I went for a long walk today, and at the beginning of it I believed that my brain, surely, could come up with a solution to this particular problem. That if I just thought about it enough and from enough different angles, then somehow, magically maybe, I would have the answer. And...well. It didn't work."

Three dots appeared with Claire's name above them, then disappeared. The same thing happened two more times before a new message appeared.

"Hazel, I know the whole 'my brain can find an answer if I just think this to death' thing feels like...well, it feels like a major perk of having a good brain, I guess. But, from here, at least, it sounds a lot more like anxiety. Like you're torturing yourself with future problems and possibilities rather than letting some natural unfolding happen."

Another message came through.

"And I get it. I really do. I know it's easier said than done to not feel something you don't want to feel. Just...please try, okay? Remember that you aren't just a tumbleweed, tossed about by the whims of the men in your life. You have agency. You are a main character."

And then, a message from Jack.

"A tumbleweed?"

Claire again.

"I don't know, Jack. I was typing quickly. Couldn't think of something else that's really light and gets tossed around by the wind."

Jack: "Well, you're the writer, I guess…"

Claire sent an eye roll emoji next.

"Oh, please. This is a first draft. If I wrote that, I would fix it in subsequent edits. For now, though, you're missing the point, I think."

Jack: "I know. I was trying to lighten the mood because you were taking Hazel to church. In a good way, of course. Speaking of which…Haze? You still there?"

Hazel was already typing her response.

"I am. And thanks, Claire. I'll think about what you said. Well…I'll try not to think about it *too* much, but you know what I mean. Maybe this isn't something I'm going to be able to figure out, but maybe it's still something I can enjoy. Somehow."

Jack was the first to respond, with another message from Claire right on the tail of his.

"Thatta girl. You can do this, sis. Try to be more like me…less thoughtful, more impulsive and bull-headed."

"We love you, Hazel. And it's all going to be okay, even if it doesn't feel much like it right now. Don't be a tumbleweed. Feel your roots."

Hazel sniffed as she tucked her phone back into her purse. She knew Claire was right, of course, even felt a bit embarrassed at realizing that she had fallen into her old ways again. She may have traded in her unrequited crush for a relationship that was its 180 degree opposite, but she was still making the same mistake. She was still letting her happiness—and in particular, her future prospects for happiness—be dictated by the main man in her life.

And sure, Oliver is a better choice, and at least we're in an actual relationship, she thought, *but I can't let myself fall apart this much just because things might go back to the way they were before I even knew him.*

As another thought occurred to her, she felt her eyes go wide. *I also don't have to accept anything as a given. Not distance or time or any of the other variables we learned about in science class. I don't have to give up on someone who means so much to me, just because his home is far away from mine. Let him not be the cause of my happiness, but also don't let my own brain and limitations convince me that happiness is impossible.*

It wasn't a solution. If anything, it was a glorified pep talk that left her just as confused as she had been before the messages she had exchanged with her brother and Claire.

But still, there was a shift, even if it was almost imperceptible. For the first time that day, she felt something solid within her, something that would endure no matter what came next. There was a part of her, a place inside her, that was strong and steadfast and carried on, no matter what was happening to the rest of her. And no, she didn't know what tomorrow held—and she certainly didn't know what the day after tomorrow would bring. But she knew that today, tonight, she had a free evening to celebrate being with the man she loved, and it had to be enough to be able to enjoy that for what it was.

She couldn't fall apart the way she had been so tempted to. As she looked around the room and spotted Zoe and Nora's children playing together, the reality of her situation sank in even more deeply.

When she looked at those children—especially the two girls, remembering being that age herself—and when she thought of her classroom back in the city, she wanted so much more for those children's futures than just love stories and happy endings.

She wanted them to have friends and work that was meaningful to them and books they loved reading and favorite bands whose concerts would be the most fun they'd ever have. Of course, she wanted them to know love and being held and safe and treasured...but it wasn't the only thing that mattered.

Seeing the simple joy on the children's faces as they chased each other around the tables—the sheer energy of their sugar-fueled game did give her a pang of sympathy for the parents involved—was the last reminder she needed. She wanted to feel whatever joy was available to her tonight, not to brace for the sadness tomorrow might bring.

Hazel set off in search of Oliver, who must have gotten lost on his way to the table covered in champagne flutes and hors d'oeuvres. She slipped her purse under her arm and began to circulate around the room, craning her neck to try to find him.

The first person to stop her was Mr. Schuler. "My dear," he greeted her, bowing and kissing the back of her hand like the old-fashioned gentleman she had known he was within seconds of meeting him. "Thank you so much for honoring us with your presence. It's been wonderful having you here, and I'm very glad that Oliver brought you as his plus one."

"Thank you, Mr. Schuler." She smiled at him. "I actually came with Daniel." At the scandalized look that appeared on his face, she hurried to explain. "Daniel and I are old friends. I didn't know Oliver before coming to Antalya, but I'm very grateful to have met him here." She leaned towards the older man, dropping her voice. "I suppose I have you to thank for that. You were a matchmaker of sorts for us, you know. If you hadn't arranged this trip—and if you hadn't generously made it possible for your employees to bring their families and plus ones—then that might never have happened." She dropped into a curtsy. "So thank you, sir."

Mr. Schuler laughed, clearly tickled, as he patted the top of her hand. "Oh, you are very welcome. I'm glad to see you two kids find each other. Apparently, it isn't an easy thing to do these days, you know. In my day, it was easy enough to meet your future spouse. I met my wife at the library, but my daughter tells me that isn't how it works anymore. She met her husband on the computer, God rest him, and I don't even want to bring up to her that maybe she should meet someone new. That it would be good for the kids to have a father figure in their life." He shook his head. "She'll just say it's too soon, and I know what she means. I can't imagine what I would do if I lost my Glenda."

His gaze went faraway as he trailed off, loving eyes aimed at his wife of sixty years. Hazel patted his hand back. "Well, that's a good reminder for you and me both to seize the day and hold on tight to the ones we love." She gestured to the room. "That's what I'm trying to do, actually. You haven't seen Oliver around, have you?"

Mr. Schuler shook his head, finally releasing her hand. "No, but I'm sure you'll find him. And I had better go give my wife a little squeeze. Happy New Year, Hazel. I truly hope this isn't our last meeting."

"I'm sure it won't be. Happy New Year, Mr. Schuler."

The next person Hazel found on her search for Oliver was Daniel. His eyes went wide as he took her in, then he hurried to pull her in for a hug. "You look beautiful, Haze! I can't believe I haven't seen you yet." He gestured vaguely behind him. "It's been...well, it's been a crazy evening, to be honest. Minnie had a wardrobe malfunction, and I was searching all over the hotel for a sewing kit, which was a harder quest than I think I'm qualified for. And then Nora was putting out fires—no, not literal ones. It's just that Zoe and Charlie learned that they had the same book—you would think, oh yay, fun, right?" He shook his head. "But no, they learned that only after they were both tugging on it from either end, practically ripping it in half. Nora had to practically do a hostage negotiation to save the book from certain doom, and then she had to convince both kids to eat some protein to hopefully ease the effects of all the sugar a little bit."

He let out a sigh. "Anyway, while all that was going on, I had to learn how to repair a broken zipper with my trusty sewing kit. It took a few YouTube tutorials, and I stabbed my finger once or twice." He held up his finger, which was covered with a SpongeBob bandage. "Anyway, as you've no doubt noticed, the entire Schuler family is fully clothed, which means my sewing endeavors were a total success."

Hazel laughed, a watery quality to it, as she pulled Daniel towards her for another hug. "It sounds like you've been having a fun evening," she said. "And I'm glad to see you so happy."

"Thanks." Concern crossed his features as he took her in. "What's going on with you? Where's Oliver?"

Hazel waved a dismissive hand. "I'm looking for him now, and I'm okay. Let's talk about it later, okay? Maybe tomorrow?" She nodded, prompting him to do the same. "Happy New Year, Daniel."

"Happy New Year, Haze."

Finally, finally...when Hazel stepped out of the restaurant into the lobby, she found Oliver sitting on a couch there, two full champagne flutes in his hands as he stared at the floor.

"Oliver," she breathed, relief flooding her senses as she took a seat next to him. "There you are."

"Here I am." He held up the glasses, giving her a weak smile. "I got the champagne."

She nodded. "I see that. You forgot to come back to me, though."

He swallowed. "I tried, but I couldn't stop thinking about what you had said before, about the unknown and about how impossible all of this seems..." He trailed off.

"And I'll admit I got to feeling a little sorry for myself." One side of his mouth raised in a smile that had no mirth behind it. "I do this cool trick now where, when I'm feeling sad or down about literally anything, I remind myself that everything would be so much easier and better if my grandmother were still around." He shook his head. "And I know it's absurd. I still felt negative feelings when my grandma was alive. And it wasn't even as if I would share all of those feelings with her. She wasn't my therapist, or anything like that. But I guess, just by reminding myself that she's gone and that that's the thing I should really be sad about, I can make myself feel worse for being sad about anything other than her death." His laugh was watery. "It doesn't make sense, I know. But it's a great way to dig myself even deeper into my misery."

"It sounds like it." Hazel leaned on his shoulder, wishing she could take away just a drop of the sadness he was feeling. She took one of the glasses from him, then took his free hand in hers. "It's okay to be sad about two different things at once, even if one of them feels so much bigger than the other one." She squeezed his hand. "But for tonight, at lest, let's enjoy what we have. Smoke 'em if you got 'em, or some other equally apt life philosophy."

Oliver chuckled as he nodded, then pushed himself to his feet, hauling her along with him. He raised his glass, and she raised hers in turn to meet it. "In that case," he said, "then here's to tonight. May the new year be a heck of a lot brighter than the old one."

"Hey now." She quirked an eyebrow. "This year had some moments I'm quite fond of. Like every moment we got to spend together. I'll take even more of those in the new year, please."

Twenty-Three

The dance floor had opened soon after Hazel and Oliver's toast in the lobby, and it was a welcome change of pace to lose herself in the loud music, in swaying to the slow songs with him, rather than continuing to talk about their problem that couldn't be solved. During the more upbeat numbers, he spun her around the dance floor, grins plastered on both of their faces as they laughed at themselves. During the slow songs, Oliver embraced her like he wouldn't let her go, and she let herself live in that delusion for as long as it would last.

When the countdown to the new year came, the music was turned down, and they all chanted the numbers. When they hit the one and cheered, shouts of "Happy New Year" filled the room, and Oliver pulled Hazel's chin towards his, kissing her squarely on the mouth. The music had stopped, but she could feel both of their hearts beating as strongly as the bass had been just a moment before. Her ears were ringing, either from the sudden absence of upbeat pop tunes or from the nearness of Oliver, the blood rushing through her veins, the perfect, almost manic joy of it all.

Before she realized what was happening, Oliver was wiping a single tear from her cheek, then kissing her again. "Happy New Year, Hazel," he whispered.

"Happy New Year, Oliver," she replied, finally taking her turn to be the one to drop a kiss on his lips. "I love you."

The high couldn't last forever—were there any highs that could, after all?—but Hazel and Oliver held on for as long as they could, finally retiring to their respective rooms a few short hours after the new year had dawned.

She didn't want to say good night to him, would have readily followed him right back to his room like a lovesick puppy, and yet she made herself stand on her own two feet, unlock her own room's door, and slip inside after dropping one more kiss on his lips. "I'll see you in the morning," she whispered.

Daniel wasn't back yet, and Hazel smiled at the thought of her oldest friend having the time of his life, partying far later than she had known him to do since they were probably in high school. She took advantage of having the room to herself, changing out of her fancy dress and washing the makeup off her face before opting to draw herself a bath. She wasn't going to fall asleep anytime soon, her mind buzzing with the noise and emotion of the evening and keeping her far from sleep, so she may as well let the hot water relax the muscles that were sure to be sore tomorrow from dancing more than she had in years.

Just as she was contemplating getting out of the bath sometime in the relatively near future, she heard the door of the room open, Daniel stumbling inside then letting out an audible, "Huh" when he found the light on and her bed empty.

"I'm in the bath," she called. "Be out in a second."

She drained the tub, got dressed in her pajamas, and reemerged, ready to debrief the evening with her friend. Daniel, still in his suit, had sprawled across his bed and was grinning up at the ceiling. He pulled himself up to sitting when she entered, directing that smile at her.

"That was a great night," he said. "Best New Year's Eve in a long time." He frowned slightly. "Happy New Year, by the way. Don't think I said that to you yet."

"I'm pretty sure you did, but not since the calendar switched over to the new page. So Happy New Year to you too, Daniel."

He folded his legs underneath himself and studied her. "Do you want to talk about whatever is bothering you? Something about you and Oliver living in different cities?"

Hazel groaned. "Not particularly. Unless you might happen to have a magical solution up your sleeve. A way to get him to New York?" She shook her head as soon as she said it. "I couldn't even ask that of him. It's way too soon, for one thing, and his entire family is in Detroit. He's going to want to be near them, especially after just losing his grandmother."

"Huh. Makes sense." Daniel nodded, then a puzzled expression crossed his face. "I know I had a lot of champagne tonight, but my brain feels like…like there's another problem looking for a solution and that these two things might align somehow." He shook his head. "Or else it's just déjà vu. Did we talk about this before? Someone wanting to get out of a city because it was too painful?"

"No." Hazel moved her head from side to side. "Oliver didn't say anything like that, and I'm sure I didn't say that. You probably talked to a lot of different people, though, so maybe it was one of them?"

"Hmm." Daniel shook his head. "To be honest, I mostly talked to one person. Nora. I'll probably deny this tomorrow when I'm totally sober, but she might just be the coolest person I've ever met." He held up a hand to stop the protest that Hazel didn't make. "I know she's grieving, and I'm not about to make a move on a widow. I'm not a total scumbag, Haze. I only pretend to be one on stage sometimes." He hoisted himself to his feet then, jerking his head toward the bathroom. "Maybe in the morning I'll be able to think a little more clearly, figure out that problem for you. But you and Oliver, you're going to be okay, one way or the other. Don't give up on it."

Hazel nodded. "I actually wasn't planning on it. Oh, I was definitely stressing about not knowing how it was all going to work, but I'm not going to admit I'm beaten until I'm actually beaten."

"And you won't be." Daniel shot her a finger guns gesture before heading towards the bathroom. "Because my Hazel never gets beaten."

She climbed under her covers, hoping Daniel wasn't wrong as a restless night stretched before her.

Hazel woke with a groan the following morning, an unwelcome stream of light hitting her retinas far too early. She blinked a few times before finding the cause of the offense, Daniel standing in front of the window, curtains flung wide open and the morning sun reflecting off a nearby window.

"What the heck, Daniel?" she grumbled, pulling the covers over her head. "What is wrong with you? Doesn't your body process alcohol like a normal human body does and shouldn't you be...I don't know...*severely* hungover right now?"

"Apparently not." She could hear the grin in his voice even without seeing it, and she gripped the blankets tighter, predicting accurately that soon he would start trying to pull them off her head. "Get up," he said. "We've got a love dilemma to solve, Haze. It's good news. You're going to want to hear this."

That got her attention. She sat up in bed, rubbing her eyes and still wishing the room were just a bit darker despite being cautiously optimistic about what Daniel might have to say. "You're not serious," she said, looking at him with a quizzical gaze. "Or else you're still tipsy. Or else I'm still asleep."

Now that she was sitting upright and her head was uncovered, Daniel started to tug on her ankle. "All of those things could be true. Well, except for the me not being serious one. It's good, Hazel. Trust me. I mean, it's not a readymade solution, but it's definitely a pathway to one." He tugged again on her ankle. "Come on. Get up, get dressed, do something about your hair. She's waiting in the cafe."

No matter how much she asked, she couldn't get any more information out of Daniel. He just crossed his arms over his chest and shook his head, occasionally changing it up by miming zipping his lips shut and throwing away the key. There was nothing to do then but go along with it, it seemed.

From her suitcase, she found a pair of jeans, a clean t-shirt, an old favorite Fleetwood Mac thrift find worn from years of wear, and a cardigan. She brushed her teeth, threw her hair into a messy bun—with the word 'messy' doing some very heavy lifting in that phrase—and splashed water on her face.

When she emerged from the bathroom, almost fully back to herself, Daniel grabbed her wrist and pulled her towards the door. She speed walked behind him all the way to the lobby, out of breath from the early morning exertions after the late night, the alcohol, and all the feelings that had only compounded it.

As they entered the cafe, her question of who this mysterious *'she'* was that they were meeting there was answered.

It was Nora. Of course it was.

I should have known it, she thought. *Who else has Daniel been spending time with?*

Still, that didn't answer the question of what they were all doing there, what this pressing issue was that they needed to talk about, and how it could possibly present any kind of solution for Hazel and Oliver.

"Hi, Nora." Hazel raised an arm in a wave, and Nora placed her coffee on the table, standing to give each of them a quick hug of greeting.

"Thanks for coming, Hazel." Nora smiled at her before directing her attention to Daniel, something unspoken passing between them. At a nod from him, she kept speaking. "Daniel told me about the challenge you and Oliver are facing. I mean, I knew it would be hard for you being parted from him, but I didn't know just how bleak it felt in terms of finding a solution that would work for both of you."

Hazel nodded. "Yeah, once I realized how little you would probably want to hear about my romantic woes, I dialed that down real quick." She gave her a close-lipped smile. "Sorry again about that."

"Don't be." Something flashed in Nora's eyes. "It made me realize something when Daniel told me about it. He was trying to remember if it was me who had said something about how hard it was to be in New York, how everything there reminded me of my late husband." She swallowed, wrapping her hands around her mug as if she were taking warmth from it. "And of course it was." She chuckled just once. "I don't think there are any other widows on the trip, so it was probably a safe bet that it was me."

"I didn't want to assume," said Daniel. "I was wearing my champagne goggles, after all, and you shouldn't exactly trust your memories when you're wearing those."

Nora nodded. "I appreciate that. You know I do. But the fact remains that I'm the one who, now that we're here and thousands of miles away from home, probably has felt like myself for the first time in months. I've been able to smile, even to have a little bit of fun..." She shot a shy glance at Daniel.

"And my kids." She sighed. "Well, they've finally gotten the version of me that they deserve again. It's not that I don't love New York. It's just that loving New York is so closely entwined with loving Thomas that I feel like a shell of myself every time something reminds me of him." She shook her head. "And everything does. Every place is a restaurant we went to together, a bench we sat on sipping coffee, a subway we rode to a party..." She trailed off, her voice smaller when she started speaking again.

"And our home. That's the hardest part of it all. There isn't a square inch of it that doesn't have him written all over it. And I know someday it will give me comfort. It will feel more like a hug to be in a place that he used to live in with me." She paused to brush something off her cheek. "But I'm not there yet. And it's going to take some more time before I can get there."

Hazel nodded. "Of course. I can't imagine anyone expects you to be able to do that." She hesitated, not sure where this all was going. "So what was it...?"

Nora let out a humorless bark of a laugh. "Why am I sharing all of this and how is it supposed to help you? Good question." She leaned forward. "It's a little known fact that I'm here on this trip not only because I am Mr. Schuler's daughter, but also because I am an employee of the Schuler Group." She blinked slowly. "That's right, a real life nepo baby right in front of you. Of course, I like to think I got the job at least in part because I'm a trained accountant, and not just as an excuse for Daddy to give me a paycheck." She pulled a face. "I haven't called him Daddy since I was younger than my kids are now, and I regretted that as soon as it came out. Please forget I said that."

"Wow." Hazel sat back, taking it all in. "Oh, I'm not re-acting to the Daddy thing." She shook her head. "I literally already forgot you said that. I'm just...I didn't realize you and Oliver had the same role. I guess that makes you work on the same team, even if you're actually hundreds of miles apart."

Nora nodded. "That's right. I've been a bit MIA from the team these last few months, but before that, we worked together quite closely." She paused. "So, the thing I'm thinking—and I know it isn't up to you, but I wanted to share it with you first—is about offering Oliver my spot in the New York office."

"What? But—?" Hazel gaped at the woman. "But why would you do that? I mean, I know what you said about it being too painful to be in New York. That all makes perfect sense. But you would give up your job? Where would you go?"

"She was thinking of switching places with Oliver if he was up for it, right Nora?" Daniel was looking at her expectantly. "Just for a year, maybe, and then you could reevaluate after that. It could be like a work exchange."

Nora's nod was hesitant, almost evasive. "Something like that, yeah. Maybe." She let out a deep sigh. "I just know I need to get out of the city and I need to get my kids out of the city. I haven't brought it up to my parents yet, but I'm sure they'd be supportive. Especially if someone capable like Oliver was coming in to fill my shoes." She pulled her lower lip into her mouth. "What do you think he would say? Do you think he would be up for it?"

Hazel didn't know what to say. She wanted to believe that Oliver would jump at the chance, but the fact was that this was all still so new and there were other factors at play, other things she didn't know how they would measure up. What about his family? His friends? What if he played in a local sport league and didn't want to let his team members down?

"I...I don't know," she said finally. "But I think all we can do is ask him. It should be up to him."

"Definitely." Nora nodded like Hazel had passed a test. "We'll have a meeting with him and my dad after breakfast." She gave Hazel a reassuring smile. "You should be there too."

Twenty-Four

Hazel was nervous throughout breakfast, her right leg jiggling as she moved her food around her plate.

"You okay?" Oliver asked, leaning over to look at her with concern. "That champagne not sitting right?"

"No, I'm good." She shook her head. "Just not that hungry this morning."

"I know what you mean," he said, lifting a scone to his mouth and taking a healthy bite. After he had chewed it, he kept speaking. "I can't help but be a little apprehensive about being called out for a meeting with the big boss. And on a holiday, of all things." He reached over and squeezed her knee, giving her a reassuring wink. "At least you were invited, too. It can't be anything too terrible if we're both there together, right?" And then, as if a thought had just occurred to him, his face blanched. "What if they're going to tell us we did something that nulled and voided the terms of the trip and now we have to pay the entire thing back? They wouldn't do that, would they?"

Hazel chuckled. The one good thing about keeping a secret from Oliver was that she knew exactly what was coming and, for once, couldn't be wept away by the same anxieties that were currently plaguing him. On any other day, being summoned by an authority figure would have her quaking in her proverbial boots. Today, though, she was simply looking forward to having a cup of coffee with Mr. Schuler and finding out if her fortune was about to change.

"I'm sure it's fine," she reassured him, patting his hand that was still resting on her leg. "Mr. Schuler is too nice and too conscientious to do something cruel right after breakfast. Plus, I read and reviewed the full terms and conditions of this trip when I signed the waiver, and I can say quite confidently that we have done nothing whatsoever that would void them."

"That's good." He breathed a sigh of relief.

"Out of curiosity, what did you think we had done, exactly?" Hazel took a bite of toast, chewing as she waited for him to respond.

He gestured vaguely. "Oh, you know...just about anything. When I saw we were summoned for a meeting with the boss, suddenly I was back at sixth grade camp, where I definitely would have gotten into trouble for kissing a girl. There was a pretty strict no fraternization policy at Camp Chuckles." He nodded, as if he was reassuring himself. "Of course, this is different. We are adults, and we didn't do anything wrong."

"No, we definitely didn't," she agreed. "Just relax as much as you can and eat your breakfast. We'll find out soon enough."

The meeting was to take place in Mr. Schuler's private suite, and Hazel and Oliver made their way there after their dishes had been cleared. As they walked hand in hand to the door, the sound of a throat clearing turned their attention behind them.

"Daniel," said Oliver, his smile turning down in surprise at the unexpected member of their party. "Are you going to Mr. Schuler's, too?" And then, looking past Daniel, he spotted the final member. "And Nora?" He shot a glance at Hazel. "What is going on here? Do you all know something about this already?"

Hazel patted his arm as they all continued on towards the door. "I don't think anyone knows exactly what's going to happen in there, Oliver. The parts I know, at least, what Nora told me...well, all of it is good. Nothing to be nervous about."

He shot her a skeptical glance. "It is alarming to me that you, the only person here who doesn't work for the Schuler Group, seem to know more about an impending work meeting than I do." He squeezed her hand. "But I trust you, so I think I can let that go."

"Good." Hazel swallowed. "For just a second there, I thought you might be mad, like I had schemed something behind your back."

"Not possible." He shook his head. "Unless, of course, you all put your heads together to come up with a really elaborate prank and I'm about to get slimed or something." He looked down on her, his expression the picture of seriousness. "That would not be okay."

"I don't think my parents know anything about sliming," chimed in Nora from behind them. "And I'd like to keep it that way. I already have the generation after me trying to make every day April Fool's Day, and I don't need it coming from the generation before me, too."

"Fair enough." Oliver pressed his lips together. "They won't hear it from me." He gestured to the door, raising his hand and nodding for their okay to go ahead and knock. When they all nodded back, he knocked three times on the wooden door.

It opened in a flash, with Mr. Schuler on the other side, already smiling. "Come on in, all!" he crowed, gesturing them inside. "Nora, your mom took the kids to the beach, so they won't be in our hair for the conversation. The kids, I mean. My lovely wife would have been a welcome addition, but it couldn't be helped."

"I could go switch out with her," Daniel offered, starting back towards the door.

"It's fine. Stay. I'll fill her in on all the details later." Mr. Schuler waved the suggestion away. "Plus, we aren't trying to turn this into a family meeting, are we Nora? It's a work meeting."

They all took seats around a coffee table, where there was a waiting carafe and a mug for each of them. As they filled their cups, doctoring them to their liking with the milk and sugar the room service staff had left there, Mr. Schuler began to speak.

"We're all here because my daughter has a proposal for us, I guess." He shot Oliver a look as he shrugged. "Your guess is as good as mine what this is about, so...well, take it away, Nora, I guess."

And so, with a deep breath to summon her strength, Nora began to explain her situation, all that she had shared with Daniel and Hazel just a couple of hours before. She talked about her late husband, her children, her desperate need for a change of scenery, and her role at the company.

They all listened, rapt, no one butting in to ask any questions or divert the conversation. And as she spoke, Nora seemed to ease, to sink into it a little more deeply. It was as if she had been carrying around this unease and uncertainty for too long, not knowing how to express it to her dad or even to herself, and now that it was all out in the open, she was feeling lighter.

She turned her attention to Oliver then. "That's why I asked to have you here, Oliver. I'm going to need to step away from my role with the company, and I think you would be the very best candidate to fill it."

"Me?" Oliver's gaze darted to Hazel, to Mr. Schuler, and then back to Nora. "You want me to take your position in the New York office?"

"Yes...you do?" Mr. Schuler asked his daughter, confusion written on his features. "Oh, it's not that Oliver isn't good at his job. He's one of the best, and I'd have transferred him to New York in a heartbeat if I didn't already have you there, Nora, holding down the fort. But if Oliver comes to New York, then what are you going to do?"

Daniel spoke up then, clearing his throat first. "Well, er...didn't we talk about—if Oliver is amenable to it, of course—you and Oliver switching places?" He raised an eyebrow at Nora. "You and your family could spend some time in Detroit, see how you all feel after six months or a year."

The smile Nora gave Daniel was tinged with so much sadness that Hazel had to divert her gaze. "I considered it," she said, "but I don't think that's the best option for all of us. I was looking at the kids this morning, at how they're flourishing here because we're so far out of our normal routine and because I'm so different from how I am back home. I think I owe it to them to make some drastic changes. To do whatever I can do to give them their mom back."

"And what are you proposing you do, Nora?" Mr. Schuler asked, lifting his coffee to take a sip.

She shrugged. "I'm not sure yet, not exactly. I think maybe we could go abroad. Spend some time in Scotland, Ireland...see some of the world." She swallowed. "I have the life insurance payout, and I can't think of anything Thomas would want more than his children getting to live their lives to the fullest."

Mr. Schuler nodded, sniffling slightly at the mention of his late son-in-law. He reached over to pat Nora's hand. "We can talk more about this later, my dear. But your mother and I will support you and your children in any way we can. I hope you know that."

"I do, Dad. Thank you." Nora's eyes were full of tears.

Daniel was the next to speak, and when Hazel turned to look at him, she felt her stomach bottom out at the crestfallen expression on his face. "You're going to leave, Nora? Of course you have to do what's right for your family. I just..."

Nora smiled sadly back at him. "I know what you want from me, Daniel. And I can't give that to you. Not yet, anyway. Give me time."

Daniel swallowed, pulling himself together enough to nod at her. "A year? Will...will that be enough for you?"

She took a long sigh. "I hope so. I really do."

Mr. Schuler made a harrumphing sound. "Right! We haven't even heard from Oliver and here we are talking about next year already. What do you think about all of this, young man?"

Oliver started slightly at the sudden shift in attention back to him, a quick glance darting to Hazel before he nodded. "I am definitely interested in being in New York. I love working for the Schuler Group, and I would value the opportunity to make a lateral move like this."

Mr. Schuler waved a dismissive hand. "Oh, lateral schmateral. If you're moving across the country for us, there's going to have to be a promotion involved. That's just common sense." He gave Hazel a sly wink then. "And as much as it's a good career move for you, I'm sure your lovely lady friend wouldn't mind having you in her city, either."

Oliver reached for Hazel's hand and gave it a squeeze. "I don't think she would at all, and I'd be very happy about it, too." A flash of concerned crossed his face, his attention turning to Nora. "I hope you aren't doing all of this on account of me. I don't want you to upset your life just so I don't have to be in a long-distance relationship with Hazel."

A long-distance relationship. She felt a flush of warmth at the words, at the reminder that, even if none of this was convenient, they would have tried to find a way to make it work, and she squeezed his hand back.

Nora dismissed his concerns. "Please. You gave me the perfect opportunity to take the leap. To do the right thing and get to be celebrated for being selfless, when really what I'm doing is all about what's best for me and my kids." A small, sad laugh escaped her lips. "If anything upset my life and all the plans I had made, it wasn't you." Daniel went to put his hand on the back of her chair, but she shook her head. "I'm okay. I'm going to be okay."

"Right, then." Mr. Schuler clapped his hands, rubbing his palms together. "What other business do we need to attend here, then? Is it all settled?"

Hazel held up a finger. "If I may...?" When he nodded at her, she spoke up. "I think this is all very exciting, and I do really appreciate being invited to the meeting, so thank you for that." She turned to Oliver. "I just want to be sure that you aren't doing something that is going to make the rest of your life harder or worse somehow. If you don't want to come to New York, we can figure out a way to still be together. Maybe we can be long-distance for a while and then I can move to Michigan or we can start a new adventure in some place that's unknown to both of us." She knew she was blushing something furious, so she hurried to get the rest of her words out. "Assuming we stay together, of course. I'm not trying to plan our entire future out." She let out a nervous laugh.

"I want to come to New York." Oliver said the words with such confidence that her eyes locked on his. "I was thinking about other roles in the company or—sorry to say this Mr. Schuler, but it's true—wondering if I would need to apply for a different job. I would be absolutely honored to fill the big shoes Nora will leave behind."

"Hey, now." Nora was looking down at her feet. "They aren't that big."

"But what about your family? Your whole life in Detroit?" Hazel shook her head. "I don't want you leaving all of that for me." Her voice grew small. "I don't want you resenting me for being the reason you have to leave it all behind."

"Hey." Oliver waited for her to look at him before speaking again. "I'm not doing it just for you. Am I crazy, or did we just meet two weeks ago?" When she chuckled nervously, he continued. "I'll visit my family as often as I can, and I'm sure they'll be happy to have a place to stay in the city, especially if I get some tickets to Broadway shows."

"That's a perk of working in the New York office," Mr. Schuler chimed in. "Not enough associates take me up on it, but we get great seats for every new opening."

"Good to know." Oliver smiled. "So you see, Hazel, this works out perfectly for everyone." He reached for her hand and gave it a soft squeeze. "Especially me."

Twenty-Five

They left the meeting with assurances that there would be paperwork waiting for Oliver at the Detroit office when he went back to work. They wouldn't nail down a date for his move yet, but he expected it to happen within six weeks. "At the absolute most," he murmured into Hazel's ear. "They can try to keep me away from you for longer than that, but it won't be pretty."

On the way back to the lobby, they stopped to ask at the front desk if there was some kind of picnic equipment they could borrow.

"You know, like a blanket to sit on and maybe a basket to carry food?" Hazel asked the woman behind the counter.

"Of course, I know, ma'am." The woman smiled back at her before gesturing out the front window towards the sea. "But as you know, it's December, and it isn't exactly picnic weather."

"That's okay," said Oliver. "We're going to wear our jackets and hats, but we just want to enjoy one last day at the beach before we have to head back to some really cold weather."

Though she looked at them like they were out of their minds, when they left a minute later, they had exactly what they needed. They headed right out the door, making a beeline to the nearest market to pick up an assortment of snacks. Hazel hadn't seen this side of Oliver, a lightness about him that was so intense she almost expected him to start floating in the air like a character from Mary Poppins.

"I didn't expect any of this," he said, shaking his head as he tossed a bag of chips into their shopping basket. "Things fell into place so easily. I feel like I'm still dreaming." He held out his arm to her. "Pinch me, please, before I get so lost in this dream that waking up actually makes me die of a broken heart."

She obliged, pinching him lightly on his forearm before leaning forward to kiss him on the tip of his nose. "It's not a dream, Oliver. It's real. And uh..." She leaned back, looking at him seriously. "I'm glad this worked out easily, but that doesn't mean things will always be easy. Life will have its challenges and we may get annoyed with each other and maybe things won't even work out between us, but—"

"Maybe, but that's not likely," he cut in. "You're the one for me." He winced as soon as he said it. "That felt just as cheesy as I imagined it would to say, but I still have no regrets. And you're right. Life can be hard. It certainly has been, and it will be again. I just don't think it will be easier without you."

"Even if I'm the one who's causing your frustration?" She was teasing him, but there was something behind it, too, a new fear that was threatening to rear its head, disturbing her peace now that she was getting what she wanted. "What if we have plans to hang out, but then we can't because it's a Sunday night, and I procrastinated grading all my papers and now I need to stay at home and do that and you're left without anyone to hang out with?"

He huffed out a laugh. "Easy. I would pick up some food and come over and watch you grade papers." He tipped his head to the side in thought. "Not really. That sounded too creepy as soon as I said it. I'd still do the food part, and I'd still come over, but I'd bring a book to read. You're cute, but even that isn't compelling enough to get me to watch you grade papers."

"Good to know." She smiled up at him. "So you think we're going to be okay?"

"We're going to be better than okay. There's still a lot that we need to figure out, but we're going to do it. One day at a time."

"One day at a time."

They sat on the beach together until the sun had sunk beneath the horizon, until their snacks were only crumbs, and until Hazel's bladder was positively screaming at her to get back to the hotel *now*. It was a perfect day, though, and she didn't want it to end.

"We have to pack," said Oliver, kissing the shell of her ear. "Even you can't pack two weeks' worth of clothing in the ten minutes before the shuttle leaves for the airport. Do it tonight. You'll sleep better if it's done."

Hazel grumbled. "I know you're right, but that doesn't mean I have to like it." She snuggled in closer next to him on the blanket. "Can't we just stay here a while longer?"

"A few more minutes," he murmured. "I don't want it to end, either."

"But it's not really the end." She said the words like they were a mantra, something they both kept reminding each other as the day wore on and the end of their time in Turkey crept closer and closer. "We'll be together again in New York before we even know it."

"Hmm," he agreed, the stubble on his cheek tickling her neck. "You'll have to show me all your favorite places in the city. I'm a real country bumpkin, you know. I'm going to need a personal tour guide to help me make sense of the big city."

At that, she giggled. "You live in Detroit, Oliver. You can pretend you grew up on a farm all you want, but we know the truth."

"Okay, you got me there." He took a deep breath. "But what I'm really concerned about is whether I'll be able to make the conversion from Detroit style pizza to New York style."

She pulled back to look at him, barely able to make out his features in the darkness. "There's such a thing as Detroit style pizza? Are you sure you don't mean Chicago style?"

Oliver gasped. "I won't hear any Detroit style pizza slander, Hazel. Not even from you. And yes, it is a real thing, and it is absolutely delicious. Some day when you come to Michigan to meet my family and see where I grew up, you'll try it and then you'll eat your words."

Her pulse had quickened at the thought of taking that trip, of her relationship with Oliver being at the point where they were meeting families and sleeping in their childhood bedrooms. Of course, given that he would be living on the East Coast soon, he would probably be meeting her family in the very near future. "I would love that," she said sincerely.

"Good. And in the spirit of fairness and compromise, I'm sure New York pizza is great, too." He lowered his voice, murmuring his next words. "Don't get me started on Chicago style pizza, though. That can be our common enemy, the force against which we unite. The entire backbone of our relationship."

"Hey, now. I like Chicago pizza. I've never met a pizza I didn't like, actually."

He groaned. "Well, there goes the backbone of our relationship. Thanks a lot, Hazel." He pulled her closer, kissing her on the cheek. "Somehow, we'll manage."

Hazel hadn't seen Daniel since the morning's meeting, and when she finally entered her room to find him there, already packed, she knew instantly that something was wrong. He was sitting on his bed, suitcase at his feet, staring blankly at a non-existent spot on the wall.

"Daniel?" she asked as she dropped her key card on the wardrobe. "Are you okay?"

"She's leaving," he said. "She's really leaving." He shook his head. "I...I thought..."

"Ah." Hazel slipped off her shoes as she stepped towards him, sitting down next to him. "Nora. You really like her, and now she's going to be on the other side of the world."

He turned to look at her, nodding. "I could handle the thought of her being in Detroit. I was already thinking of using my frequent flier miles to visit her there." He shook his head. "But she doesn't want that. Of course she doesn't. She's grieving, for crying out loud. She's not looking for a new man in her life. And I..." He trailed off, his eyes searching Hazel's. "I wasn't trying to be her new man. Wasn't trying to replace her husband or swoop in and be her kids' new dad. I just..."

"You really liked being around her," she said. "And you were good for her. I could see that. She looked lighter when she was around you. Happier, almost." She swallowed, searching for her next words. "Maybe she just needs time, you know? She needs time to heal and to focus only on her children and then...well, who knows what happens next, after that."

Daniel nodded. "Yeah. I think it could be really good for all of them, taking a year to see the world, to focus on the good things, to process their loss." He swallowed. "I'm going to miss them all, though. Minnie and Charlie, they're really good kids. And at that age, they change so fast, you know? What if they don't even remember me when they come back?"

"They will," Hazel reassured him. "They aren't babies, Daniel. They have object permanence, and they will remember you even when you aren't with them."

"What if they don't come back?" He practically breathed the question. "What if they all start a new life in Scotland or something?"

She sighed. "Then you'll find a way to be happy that they're happy. And you'll move on."

"I know." He closed his eyes. "I don't have a claim on any of them. I have to let them go."

"You do."

"And if they come back to me..."

Hazel smiled. "Then you never have to let them go again."

"Thanks, Haze," he said, smiling at her. "I hope it all works out for me as well as it did for you."

"I hope so too, Daniel." She bumped her shoulder into his. "Speaking of which, look at us. Who would have thought we'd be sitting here like this, talking about our love lives?"

"I know. You're pretty amazing, you know that?"

"Right back at you, bud."

He looked around the room, at the mess of her clothing that had expanded to take up more space than even seemed possible based on the size of her luggage. "You'd better start packing, though. I am not missing our flight because of you, no matter how much I'd rather stay here in Turkey than go back and face the music in New York."

"We're not going to miss our flight." She rolled her eyes. "We have, what...like six hours before we need to head to the airport? Watch me get this done in way less time than that. It'll take..." She surveyed the room, pretending to do the math in her head. "...five and a half hours at most."

They said goodbye to the hotel the following morning, with promises to Elliot, Anya, and Zoe to meet up soon in the city for brunch. Oliver had given both Daniel and Hazel hugs, along with instructions to start planning the itinerary for his first days in the city, when they were to be his tour guides.

Hazel had held back, enjoying a few more moments by Oliver's side while Daniel said goodbye to Nora and her children. Nora had made the hard-won decision not to go back to New York at all, but to begin her international adventure with her kids as soon as possible. Her parents had already made arrangements to pack up the things they would need and send them over, a few spare boxes of the most essential items that would be awaiting them at their first stop.

"So they're really doing it then," said Oliver, his eyes on Nora and her family. "Good for them."

Hazel nodded. "It is. I think it might be good for Daniel too, even if it doesn't feel that way now." She continued to watch her old friend, a soft smile forming on her face as she thought about how far they had come. Feeling Oliver's eyes on her, she looked up into his face. "What?"

He shook his head. "I'm just so amazed by you, by the way you've changed here. You aren't having mixed feelings about Daniel falling for someone?" He cleared his throat softly. "I would understand if you did. I mean, I'm not asking because I'm jealous or anything, just because I can't imagine how you could get over him like that and how it could be so final."

She wrapped her arms around his waist and gave him a squeeze. "It was easy. I found the real thing, and I lost my taste for the substitute. Kind of like what's about to happen to you when you taste New York pizza for the first time," she teased. "No, but seriously." Her expression sobered. "You made it so clear to me that there was a very significant difference between the love of a friend and the love of, well…your person. I love Daniel as a friend, and I want him to be happy. And you? Well, you I just love. Just as you are. Just as I am."

His smile was pure bliss. "I love you too, Hazel."

Twenty-Six

Eleven Months Later

It was the night before Thanksgiving, and Hazel was back in the hometown bar she and Jack used to visit every year during college when they came back home. It was the place to be for a version of a high school reunion, but she was pleased to see that, now that it was more than a decade since she had graduated, there were fewer familiar faces and the bar was crowded with people who were clearly more recent graduates.

It wasn't that she didn't want to see any of her old classmates; it was just that she had everyone she needed right there at her table, and she didn't want to have to divide her attention with anyone else. She leaned against Oliver's shoulder, his solid presence just as reassuring as it had been from the very beginning of their relationship. She smiled across the table at Claire, who was outlining her upcoming book tour and all the stops it entailed.

"And you're going too, Jack?" she asked her brother, taking a sip of her beer.

Jack nodded. "Of course. The chance for us to go back to Munich together, to where it all began, would be reason enough. But getting to join Claire for the whole thing will be really fun, I think. We'll get to see Emma and Connor again when we go to Ireland, and I'll finally get to visit the Emerald Isle." He wasn't quite meeting her eye, and if she wasn't imagining it, his cheeks had gone fully pink. She made a mental note to corner her brother later and ask him if he might, perhaps, have some plans for this European book tour that involved an engagement ring and an important question.

"You guys will be back for Christmas?" she asked. "Mom and Dad threatened us with bodily harm if we didn't spend it with them, so I'm sure you got that same threat."

Jack nodded. "Oh, definitely." He shrugged. "If the airline messes up again, though, it can't be helped."

"We won't be volunteering to take the later flight this year," said Claire, rolling her eyes at her boyfriend. "One holiday spent in a hotel is more than enough, thank you very much. Yes, of course, I'm grateful that we got to meet there, but this year I'd rather have matching Christmas pajamas and sleep in my own bed."

"Whatever you say, dear." Jack kissed the side of her head, then grinned across the table at his sister like he had won the lottery.

"I...uh, well I think I'm going to be the only one spending Christmas abroad this year, then," the fifth person at their table spoke up, and Hazel turned to take in Daniel, who wasn't quite meeting her gaze.

"Oh, yeah?" She felt Oliver applying gentle pressure on her knee and dialed down the intensity just a bit. "Where are you going?"

"Oh, just...well, I was thinking I might meet up with Nora and her kids. She, uh...she invited me, and I mean, I don't have any other plans, so...yeah. I might do that."

The only thing that stopped Hazel from clapping her hands together and squealing with glee was Oliver grabbing her hand under the table. When she looked up at him, he pressed his lips together and gave her the barest shake of his head.

"That sounds great, Daniel," said Oliver, speaking for both of them. "Please give Nora our best."

"Oh, and the kids, too!" Hazel chimed in. "How are they? Has it been a good year? Where are they?"

Daniel held up a hand. "I...probably don't know any of the answers to the questions you just asked," he admitted. "I mean, I know they're good enough to be inviting an extra person to join them for the holidays, so I'm hoping that's a good thing. But to be honest, as soon as she asked, I just said yes. I'll figure all the rest of it out soon."

"Yeah, man, it would probably be good to know which country you're flying to before you book a plane ticket," said Jack, chiming in like the surrogate older brother that he was to Daniel.

"I will," said Daniel. He fixed his sights on Hazel and Oliver, seeming eager to get the focus off of himself and back somewhere safer. "So, what are your plans for the holidays? Haze, are you finally going to go meet Oliver's family in person?"

"Yes!" Hazel crowed. "I've met them on the phone, but it'll be great to finally see them in their full-size form. We're going to be here for Christmas, do the whole pizza making tradition with these two"—she gestured to Jack and Claire—"and then we'll be in Michigan for New Year's Eve. We'll probably do the opposite next year."

"Sounds like a great plan," said Daniel, tracing a line of condensation down the side of his glass. "The perfect way to keep both sides of the family happy."

Jack cleared his throat and held up his glass. "I'm going to make a toast," he announced, and they all lifted their glasses in unison.

He looked at Claire, then across at Hazel and Oliver, finally tracking his eyes on Daniel. "Here's to a Christmas themed love story," he said. "In my book, those are the best ones."

"Oh, definitely," said Claire.

"Can't argue," said Hazel, smiling up at Oliver who nodded back at her.

"Alright, alright," said Daniel, sighing. "You've all made your stances clear. I'll do my best to get a Christmas love story of my own just as soon as I can."

And with that, they all clinked their glasses together, the next sip of their beverages going down even sweeter.

Author's Note

Thank you so much for joining me for another Christmas story. This series has been one of my absolute favorites to write.

The next (and, at this point, last) story in the series will feature Daniel and Nora, and will be published in 2025.

To stay updated on other works in progress, please visit my website at kcmccormickciftci.com.

If you loved this book, please consider leaving a review, as that is one of the best ways to support indie authors like me. Reviews left on major retail sites (wherever you bought this book is a great start!), Goodreads, and Book-Bub will help other readers discover this book, too.

About the Author

KC McCormick Çiftçi is an English teacher turned romance writer. She spent the majority of her twenties living and working abroad, collecting the experiences that inform the stories she tells. She enjoys telling multicultural and international love stories through romantic comedy and women's fiction. She lives in Turkey with her husband and a herd of cats.

Prior to diving into the world of romance, KC published two self-help books for intercultural couples, *Loving Across Borders* and *The K-1 Visa Wedding Plan*. Both are available wherever books are sold.

For updates on upcoming releases, behind the scenes news, and all my favorite book recommendations, visit kcmccormickciftci.com (or just point your phone camera at the QR code below).

Books by KC McCormick Çiftçi

Austen in Turkey
Pride, Prejudice, & Turkish Delight
Sense, Sensibility, & the Mediterranean Sea

Home (Abroad) for the Holidays
Christmas on Inishmore
Christmas at Terminal One
Christmas by the Sea

Intoxicated by You
Intoxicated by You

Cats of Istanbul
The Vet Upstairs
From Strays to Soulmates
Whiskers and Wanderlust

Intercultural Relationship Self Help
Loving Across Borders
The K-1 Visa Wedding Plan

www.ingramcontent.com/pod-product-compliance
Lightning Source LLC
Chambersburg PA
CBHW012039140726
47991CB00011B/3196